A PLAGUE OF DEMONS

A RINEHART SUSPENSE NOVEL

Rinehart Suspense Novels
by John Creasey as Gordon Ashe

A Shadow of Death
A Blast of Trumpets
The Big Call
A Herald of Doom
Murder with Mushrooms
A Life for a Death
The Croaker
A Rabble of Rebels
Wait for Death
A Nest of Traitors
The Kidnaped Child
A Scream of Murder
Double for Death
A Clutch of Coppers
Death from Below
A Taste of Treasure

A RINEHART SUSPENSE NOVEL

A PLAGUE OF DEMONS

John Creasey
as Gordon Ashe

HOLT, RINEHART AND WINSTON
New York

Published simultaneously in Canada by Holt,
Rinehart and Winston of Canada, Limited.

Library of Congress Cataloging in Publication Data
Creasey, John.
    A plague of demons.

    (A Rinehart suspense novel)
    I. Title.
PZ3.C86153PK3   [PR6005.R517]   823'.9'12   76-4733
ISBN 0-03-017541-0

First published in the United States in 1977.

Printed in the United States of America
10   9   8   7   6   5   4   3   2   1

Contents

A PLAGUE OF DEMONS

A RINEHART SUSPENSE NOVEL

DEMON: 1. An evil spirit: devil; fiend
2. A very wicked or cruel person

1 Cruel Devils

'Don't hurt me,' she begged.

She lay, helpless and nearly naked; tied hand and foot to her own soft bed, in her room of beauty and luxury, laughter and happiness, passion and delight.

A light, vividly bright, shone into her eyes.

'Don't hurt me,' she begged.

She was not used to pain, for even the minor hurts and aches had passed her by, certainly there was none that she could remember. Love and affection, instant soothing, instant salving, instant sanctuary in need; these had been hers since childhood.

Her parents had loved her; her husband adored her, guarding and protecting her from all things that might do her harm.

'Please – please,' she begged, brokenly, 'don't hurt me – again.'

No one answered; there was no way of being sure that anyone was still there; no way of being certain that in one moment, or in ten, the devils would strike at her again, causing excruciating pain, making her scream with terror. She could see only the light, which blinded her, and the darkness beyond. She could hear nothing: no movement, no voices. She could feel the tug of cords at her wrists and ankles, and they hurt. But that was not what she meant when she pleaded. That was not true pain.

9

She lay on her back, her breath coming in short, uneven gasps.

She could not even be sure that she was in her own room, in her and Justin's lovely house, because in the intervals of freedom from pain there had been the light and the darkness and perhaps periods of unconsciousness, or semi-conscious coma, even of drugged 'sleep'. She could not be sure. Her pleading was a kind of reflex action, for her mind was beyond reason, decision, or constructive thought.

If they were not still here, why was she still bound to the bed?

If they had bound her to her own bed, and she could remember that they had, would they have unbound her and then tied the same cords in the same place on another bed?

They *must* be here.

They?

She knew there were at least two of them, and from the muttering she had heard in intervals of conscious sanity she thought she had heard several. All the voices were those of men, and all spoke in a language which she did not understand.

Why – tonight?

How had they known that Justin would not be here?

How had they known that for once, a rare occasion, the Rannikers, houseman and cook, were out for the evening and would not be back until the early hours? Their daughter was gravely ill, in childbirth, and they had been so distressed by the danger to the mother and the child and the need to leave Ursula here alone.

She had said: 'Of course you must go. I'm not frightened.'

What a lie she had known that to be.

'One of us will be back, whatever happens,' Joe Ranniker had said.

And surely he would be; soon.

Please God the nightmare was over, now, and the devils who had tortured her gone. Surely – surely they would not have stayed still for so long. They must – *surely* they must – have gone away, leaving the light to blind her with its white incandescent glare, so that tears filled her eyes and fell slowly down her cheeks and even trickled to her lips where she could taste the salt of them. They had locked her head in some way, she couldn't turn it, could not look away, could not hide from the glaring white.

Suddenly, it went out.

Every nerve in her body seemed to scream.

At first, despite the darkness, light was still harsh against her eyes, but slowly there came only the darkness. Utter darkness. And silence, except for her gasping breath. If the light had been put out there *must* be someone in the room, yet she could hear nothing.

Oh God! Why couldn't she stop making the rasping noise as she breathed? It drowned all other sounds. She *must* stop; must hold her breath. It was as if some great storm were fighting within her as she tried. Breath battled in her lungs and she could not keep quiet, even though her breast felt like bursting she could not keep quiet.

The breath burst out of her, and for a few moments she drew in short, shallow gulps of air which threatened to suffocate her. Everything was banished from her mind but this awful fight for survival. If she could not draw breath deeper into her lungs then not only they but her heart would burst.

Gradually, she quietened.

11

There was the darkness and the near-silence and even her own breathing was less tumultuous. It would not prevent her from hearing anything or anyone else in the room.

There was light!

Oh, dear God, there was a patch of light. It was like mist about a lamp amid a sea of darkness. Misty light. In front of her. Growing. The size of a man's head at first, but growing until now it was a huge, circular patch of mist, glowing, something unearthly, like ectoplasm. Silent. Unmoving except that it grew larger and larger.

And it drew nearer.

Her breathing became laboured and short again, but now sound did not seem to matter, all that mattered was the mist which seemed to fill the room. It wasn't natural, it couldn't be natural.

There was something in the mist: a shape.

At first it was simply darker in the centre than any-where else; a *shape*. Slowly, slowly, it became a face. A man's face. She was now so still she could hardly breathe. *It was a face*. Eyes, nose, mouth; dark head, high forehead, pointed chin. It was dark despite the light of which it was the centre.

The eyes were closed, but slowly opened; dark eyes with a shiny brightness. It was getting larger. Larger. *No!* It was drawing nearer.

She saw the lips.

They were thin, drawn up at the corners in what might be a smile, might be a sneer. *Dear God, save me, save me.* But she had never believed, not *believed* in God or the devil, or –

The face changed colour; there was a red tinge to it now and to the surrounding mist. A red glow as of fire.

12

And the features became clearer and sharper; small, pointed nose, pointed chin, pointed ears – *pointed ears*. The eyes were wide open and staring but the lips remained set.

She was lying in a bath of sweat.

Then she saw the marks on the forehead; she saw them appear, saw them grow; become larger. She did not realize at first what they were, but suddenly the lips moved in a smile for which there was only one word: demoniac. And she knew that those marks were horns.

The devil himself.

No! That was madness, there was no devil, there was no –

Pain seared through her as if some unseen hand had drawn the point of a razor-sharp knife across and across her body.

She screamed, but could hear no sound.

Without warning, the pain seared again.

Then it paused. She had no idea how long this pause lasted. She only knew that for a while her whole body was rigid in the tension of fear and expectancy. Gradually her nerves and muscles relaxed and she was able to look about her again, and to see what pain had driven into temporary oblivion.

The mist; the face; the horns; the pointed ears; she was looking into the leering face of the devil himself.

Then pain stabbed; and stabbed again; arms, legs, eyes, mouth, everywhere, until it seemed that her whole body was being devoured by flames, as if she were burning in the fiery pit of hell.

Suddenly, full oblivion came.

Had it been death she would have welcomed it.

While she lay there, inert, unfeeling, men moved

13

about the room, ignoring her, packing small cases, taking electric plugs out of the many points, making no sound except a murmured word or two. They were ready to go, three of them, when the telephone bell rang. A harsh and jarring note; it rang on and on. The three men went out, while the bell still rang into the stillness.

Ursula Franklin did not hear it.

No one heard it in the now silent house.

Sir Justin Franklin held the receiver to his ear in a large hotel in Manchester, some two hundred miles from his house in Surrey, and listened, puzzled, to the ringing sound as he called his wife. It was a little after eleven o'clock, and later than his usual call when away, but Ursula read a lot in bed and seldom put the light out until midnight. He told himself that someone might have called and taken her out, they had a host of friends and relatives, she more relatives than he. But if that had happened, why didn't the Rannikers answer? Even if they were in bed, and she were out, the telephone would be switched through to their room.

The operator came on the line with her unmistakable Lancashire accent.

'Ah'm sorry, sir, but there's still no reply.'

'Can you check if the line is out of order?' Franklin asked.

'London did that, sir, five minutes ago,' the girl said. 'Ah'll try again if – '

'No. I'll try again later,' Franklin said. 'Thank you for your patience.'

He rang off, frowning, stockinged feet up on the bed, jacket draped over a chairback because the room

14

was over-warm, a copy of the *Manchester Evening News* also folded on the bed. He scowled at the cinema advertisements to which it was opened. He had finished his business early, not looked forward to a long evening alone, run idly down the entertainments column and come upon *Dr Zhivago,* a film he had missed time and time again. He had not expected it to last for so long; he shouldn't have gone out, he should have called earlier.

More nonsense! If she were out now she would also have been so earlier.

The obvious solution to the problem would be if she had gone out and told the Rannikers that they could take the evening off also – but if that were so, why was no one back by now? He looked at his watch: it was half past eleven, he must wait a little while before he rang again.

The whole disquieting incident hardly made sense, for if she had planned to go out, she would most certainly have told him. She would not allow the house to be deserted at a time when his call would have been expected. It was 'no use pretending, there was something very odd about this, and he could not rest in peace.

It was *not* because he was jealous.

The very idea was utter nonsense! He had not the slightest reason to be jealous, the fact that he was twenty years older than Ursula did not matter, they were as much one as any two people could be. Yet – he hated going away even for a night. He hated leaving her alone. He wondered whether she had secret longings for a younger man, or at least for the company of younger people and – well, he may as well admit it, he *was* jealous. Not of anyone in particular – he had

15

not the faintest cause for that – but because of his fear of losing her.

He began to pace the room, thinking, as he had often done, that at times everything seemed perfect and at others everything seemed wrong, or potentially wrong. He worked, and much of the time lived, with older people. At forty-eight he was one of the most brilliant economists in Britain, consulted by the government, by city corporations and by big business organizations which were really empires: that was one reason why he had come here, to advise the City of Manchester Corporation. He could have been fêted, or at least wined and dined, by civic officials, but he preferred not to continue with business into the evening.

Damn *Dr Zhivago*!

Damn the committee which had brought him here!

Confound his own unreasoning, jealous heart.

There was no cause; certainly none tonight, for if she had gone out with another man she would certainly have made sure the Rannikers were at home to answer his call, to tell them whatever lie she wanted passed on.

What the devil was the matter with him?

He clenched his hands, seeing in the old-fashioned wardrobe mirror a tall, rugged-looking man with dark hair flecked with grey; a strong and powerful-looking man with clear, light blue eyes, shown up vividly by jet black eyebrows and lashes. He glared at himself, and then, swinging round, snatched up the telephone again.

There was no answer: just brrr-brrr; brrr-brrr.

He did not persist too long this time, but put the receiver down slowly, saying with great deliberation: 'I must think.' He began to move around again, talking to himself as he did so. 'I am genuinely worried.

16

This is not simply a question of senseless jealousy, it is a matter of reason. There should be an answer. Even if the Rannikers had been allowed the evening off, they would be back by now. So there is something wrong.'

He paused in his pacing and in his speaking, only to resume with almost fierce persistence:

'If there is something wrong I must find out what it is. It is too late to ask neighbours to go and check, and I don't want to send for the police. So who shall I ask?'

He stopped talking, but continued to pace the floor, deep lines etched on his forehead and a particularly deep groove appearing between his eyes. He was now addressing himself to this situation as he would to any problem of economics, and he was applying the principle in which he so deeply believed: that however complicated problems might appear to be, their solutions were simple, once the key to them was found.

He must not call on the neighbours.

He must not call on any of Ursula's relatives; they would suspect his motives.

He could not call on any of his own, for he did not trust their discretion.

He must not call on the police because a police car going to the house might be noticed and would cause talk among the neighbours.

He *could* hire a private plane and go down himself, but it would take too long; he needed the help of someone on the spot.

But who?

Quite suddenly he stopped his pacing, raised a clenched fist, and after a split second said explosively: 'Dawlish, Pat Dawlish, *he's* the man.'

17

On the instant he was at the telephone again, asking Directory Inquiries for the number of Patrick Dawlish who lived at Millbank, London SW1.

2 *Dawlish Wakes*

Patrick Dawlish was sleeping; most of those who knew him would admit that it was the sleep of the just.

He lay on one side of a huge bed, known in the United States of America as king-size and in England known hardly at all. On the other side of the bed lay his wife Felicity, who was also asleep; the sleep of the beautiful.

Dawlish wore no pyjama jacket and the tossed sheet disclosed one massive shoulder and his deep chest. Felicity, huddled beneath the bedclothes, was more susceptible to cold than her husband, though just as ready as he to have the window down a foot, and allow the sharp night air to blow across the room. They were atop one of London's tallest modern buildings, in a penthouse apartment with views which seemed to spread over the whole of London. One window faced north-east and from it one could see the bridges of the Thames, the Tower of London, St Paul's, even Big Ben's bright yellow face – and opposite Big Ben an old red brick building which had once housed the whole of New Scotland Yard, headquarters of the London Metropolitan Police Force. Today it housed offshoots of several government departments and, on the top floor, Dawlish's apartment. For he was the

Deputy Assistant Commissioner for Crime in London, and his special duty was to deal with crime which had international repercussions.

The telephone on Felicity's side of the bed rang.

Felicity Dawlish groaned in her sleep and turned over. The bell rang again. She opened her eyes and at the same time heard the bell ring for a third time.

She eased herself up in bed and stretched out for the receiver. Cold air struck at her bare arms and nearly bare shoulders. *Brrrh*! She put the receiver to her ear.

'This is Felicity Dawlish.'

'I'm sorry to worry you, Mrs Dawlish,' a man's voice said, deeply apologetic, 'but there is someone on the line who says he's an old friend of Mr Dawlish and *must* speak to him.'

'Does he give his name?'

'No – he said it was confidential. He – ah – has a very authoritative voice, Mrs Dawlish. *Is* Mr Dawlish there?'

'Sleeping so deeply he didn't hear the telephone.'

'Oh, I *am* sorry.' The speaker, one of the night staff of the office who intercepted all private calls to Dawlish's listed number – close friends used his unlisted one – knew that for three days and nights Dawlish had been at work on a case, snatching forty winks whenever he could, and had reached home early that evening utterly exhausted. 'Shall I say Mr Dawlish is not – '

Dawlish, who until that moment had lain as if in hibernating slumber, slowly moved his right arm and slid it over Felicity's shoulder, kissed her ear, and took the telephone from her.

'What is the new calamity?' he demanded.

'Oh, Mr Dawlish! I *am* sorry to disturb you, I really

19

am. This gentleman sounds in such distress but he simply won't give his name. He does, however, claim to be an old friend – he says you were at Bellamy together, and – '

'Put him through,' Dawlish decided without hesitation, and then heard a different voice on the telephone, a deep one with overtones of authority one could not mistake, though he had no memory of hearing it before.

'Is that Pat Dawlish?'

'Yes.'

'This is Justin Franklin,' the other man announced.

Dawlish knew the name was familiar, but for the moment he could not place it. Who on earth – Got it!

'Good Lord!' he exclaimed. 'Master Relativity himself.'

The other man was surprised into a laugh. Justin Franklin, the boy wonder at Bellamy's – which was a house at one of the most famous of England's public schools – who had so exasperated a succession of physics and science masters with his grasp not only of advanced physics but of Einstein's Theory of Relativity that they had dubbed him 'Master Relativity'. How cruel and yet how penetrating some nicknames could be!

All of these things passed through Dawlish's mind in a second or two, and almost as soon as the other's laugh had broken he went on:

'Trouble?'

'There might be,' Franklin said.

It must be a very strong 'might' for him so to presume on a long-dead acquaintance, even though Franklin had earned both renown and honours in the field of economics: what he called 'social' economics, or the pounds and pence of making society work. Dawlish waited, assuming that the other was marshalling his thoughts. So it proved.

'Dawlish, I may be a fool. I may be emotionally disturbed – in fact to some degree I am. But – ' He told the story with great economy of detail, enough for Dawlish to understand how he was feeling, including the possibility that he might be making a fool of himself. At last he went on: 'Can you go to my house or arrange for someone to go in plain clothes, break in and make sure all is well?'

'Yes,' Dawlish said at once. 'I'll go myself.'

'I'll be eternally – ' Justin's voice broke, but he quickly recovered. 'I'll be eternally grateful. The telephone number here is ...'

As he spoke, Dawlish repeated the Manchester number and Felicity, right hand stretched out, wrote this down on a pad which stood by the side of the telephone. As he finished repeating it, Dawlish said:

'Now, the address of your house? . . . Number 17, Pemberton Crescent, Esher, Surrey. . . . Exactly how do I get there? . . .' He repeated the directions which seemed straightforward enough, and then said: 'The odds are a hundred to one that there's nothing to worry about. I should expect a call in less than an hour and a half – half past one, say.'

He rang off on Franklin's repeated thanks, tossed back the sheet and blankets, and went into the bathroom. When he came back Felicity was coming from the door leading from the main hall with a tea tray. Tall for a woman, she was nevertheless much shorter than Dawlish. She wore an ankle-length dressing-gown which looked fluffy and warm, a gold colour which set her hair and complexion off well.

21

'Bless you,' Dawlish said. 'Not even a "must you go yourself".'

'You wouldn't do so if you didn't feel it was necessary,' Felicity said, in a matter-of-fact voice. 'Are you going alone?'

'I'll ask the Yard to have a divisional police car waiting to guide me from the end of the Kingston bypass,' he told her, 'and they can give me support if I seem to need it. Pour me out a cup, sweet.' He dialled his office number and asked the same man who had called him to make the arrangements. Then, finishing his tea, he pulled on his trousers and a polo-neck sweater, slid into a jacket, and stretched for his shoes.

'May I come?' asked Felicity.

'You don't seriously want to.'

'I don't seriously want to stay here alone for the rest of the night,' she said.

He gave a sudden, boyish grin.

'If you can be downstairs at the foyer dressed for the journey by the time I've gone round to the garage and brought the car round – *yes*.'

He pretended to leap towards the door.

Dear fool, thought Felicity. Dear, precious, gallant fool. Here was a voice out of his past and he responded as if there was not a moment's doubt about the wisdom of going; as if he had forgotten that he had slept so little in the past few days. Perhaps he *had* forgotten: she never ceased to marvel at the incredible resources of strength and tenacity he could call on.

As she moved from the subdued lighting of the foyer, dressed now in warm tweed suit and fur-lined boots, Dawlish was pulling into the carriageway. He had almost certainly waited until he had seen her coming and then moved forward.

22

At that moment Ursula Franklin lay still as death.

At that same moment Sir Justin Franklin switched off the radio in his room, sick of the pop music which was so out of tune with his own fears.

At that same moment three men were entering a house on the other side of London; near Epping.

And at that identical moment a middle-aged woman crouched at bay in a barely furnished room in an outer London suburb. She clasped her arms in a subconscious effort to hide from the three figures whom she knew were there. She was not looking at them, she was shivering with fear and sobbing.

She was perhaps fifty; or in the early fifties.

She had been dragged from her bed, stripped and beaten. Why? Why? She had never seen any of the men – if they *were* men, and not devils – before. Though how could she tell, for they had all worn masks.

She kept asking herself: *Why?*

Why should they break in here? She had no valuables, nothing worth stealing. *Why?*

One of them came towards her. She screamed 'No! No!' and, still screaming, collapsed, falling to one side.

Slowly her body went still except for trembling, broken by spasms of acute shaking and shivering. She heard a sound and after a while knew that it was her own moaning. She could hear no other sound, and gradually she began to hope.

Had they – gone?

She opened her eyes to a strange, misty light. It carried her mind back to a day in her childhood when storm and rain and sun together had filled a mountainside with ethereal light. This had the same red tinge.

There was a face, emerging, sallow, small-featured, horned, with dark hair and pointed ears. A devil's face.

23

'No!' she screamed. 'No!'

Suddenly, pain tore at her body.

'No, no, no, no!' she screamed, until the contortions of her body and the misty light and the red glow and the devil's face all seemed to merge together, and she could not distinguish between what she could hear and see and feel. After a while her screaming became soundless, as in a nightmare.

When she woke from the nightmare it was dark.

It was pitch dark.

She sobbed, but could not move.

She was stiff and sore and there was a memory of pain and of the face of the very devil himself.

'No!' she screamed.

But no one heard her because she lived alone, and there was no one to succour her, no one to reassure her when she opened her eyes.

She muttered: 'No, no, no more, no, devil, no more, devil, devil, no more.' She began to cry, as a child might cry.

But no one heard her.

3   Break-In

Dawlish pulled the Allard he was driving at that time into a parking lay-by at the Esher end of the Kingston by-pass. Here, in a countryside which had lost most of its true country nature and yet, off the highways, was pleasant and blessedly green by day, everything seemed peaceful. Lights glowed at the windows of nearby

24

houses. There was one car ahead of them in the parking place. This should be the police car.

'I don't understand why you thought it worth coming yourself,' Felicity said tentatively. 'It might be nothing at all to worry about.'

'Just one old Bellyacher to another,' Dawlish responded lightly.

She knew there was more to it than that; a hunch, perhaps, disguised as an answer to an old school friend's appeal. She felt the warmth of his hand on her own, as a man in plain clothes came hurrying from the car in front; a youthful-looking man with a spring in his step.

'Mr Dawlish?'

'Yes,' Dawlish replied.

'I'm Chief Inspector Hennessy, sir, of the Surrey CID.'

'Very glad you were so ready to help,' Dawlish said, aware that Hennessy's rather broad-featured face was set in momentary surprise at seeing a woman in the car. 'My wife came along for the ride.'

'Oh, I *see*, sir,' said Hennessy, in the voice of one who did not see at all. 'I've been along Pemberton Crescent and past Number 17 with the police officer who always goes along there at night. Everything seems normal, sir.'

'Let's hope it stays that way.'

'Will you follow me, sir? I know you're anxious not to attract any attention, so if I just flick my lights off for a moment when I'm passing Number 17 you'll know that's the house. It so happens the house next door is empty at the moment, and I and my detective sergeant can make our way across the wall between the gardens. *If* that's all right with you.'

'I can't think of a better idea,' Dawlish said. 'Will

one of your chaps stand by my car? Mrs Dawlish will be in it and we don't want anyone to run away with her, do we?'

Very funny, thought the Chief Inspector, as he said warmly: 'We certainly don't, sir.' *Could* Dawlish be a facetious ass? he wondered, with an inflated ego to match an inflated reputation? 'I'll see to it.'

'Thanks,' Dawlish said.

'Thank you, Inspector,' Felicity Dawlish said, leaning across her husband. 'My husband is really afraid I might try to run away. Aren't you, dear?' she asked mischievously.

They *haven't* been drinking, have they? Hennessy asked himself as he went back to his car. He had a driver and a detective sergeant with him and gave them instructions as they started off for Pemberton Crescent. He kept his opinions to himself, deciding to reserve judgement. The driver was the night patrol officer who knew the district well. He led the way through tree-lined avenues, past large houses standing in their own grounds, turning many corners and passing numerous dead ends, until after ten minutes Dawlish said:

'I'm glad I didn't try to find this place on my own.'

'You're never alone when I am with you,' Felicity said lightly. 'I think – look! This is Pemberton Crescent!'

A sign, painted white on a dark board, showed the name of the street clearly beneath a street lamp. Dawlish slowed down, and suddenly the lights of the car in front of them went out, coming on again almost immediately. Dawlish touched the brake and turned the wheel slightly until the dimmed headlights shone on an open gate on which the number 17 was written.

26

He turned into the carriageway.

A light shone from the porch of a house which, though large and opulent, could not be very old, for the land on which all the nearby houses were built had been virgin woodland only twenty years before. A house of this size in such a neighbourhood, Dawlish decided, must cost a fortune, both to buy and to maintain.

'Coming with me?' he asked Felicity.

'In the house, do you mean?'

'Not yet,' Dawlish answered. 'Walking round,' he added, as he handed Felicity out of the car, 'should show us what windows and doors are vulnerable and might show some evidence of whether anyone who shouldn't have been here has been. I – '

He broke off abruptly. His hand, light until that moment on Felicity's forearm, tightened like a vice. He was staring at a flower-bed newly turned, and at the driveway as it led round a corner of the house. To Felicity all this seemed normal, nevertheless Dawlish's disquiet touched her.

'See something?' she asked nervously.

Dawlish nodded grimly.

'Is there someone – '

'Something,' he said. 'Not someone.' He went forward, relaxing his grip on her arm, their shadows cast dark and long by the headlamp beams. At the flower-bed he paused. 'Do you see that?' He went down on his haunches and peered at the dark earth in which there were still the marks of a rake or fork.

There were other prints; she thought at first they were the footprints of a large dog; a *huge* dog. There were at least ten, leading from the side nearest the front door to the gravel, where they disappeared.

27

'It looks like – a pony,' Felicity said, huskily.

'A pony with a cloven hoof,' answered Dawlish.

'What – what do you mean?'

'I mean those footprints were made by man, or another two-legged animal,' Dawlish replied in a tense voice. 'They are too much in line to have been made by a four-footed beast. And they're not shoe-marks, they're more like hoof-marks.' He stood up very slowly as two men approached from the grass and trees on the far side of the drive. 'Chief Inspector?'

'Yes, sir.' Hennessy now moved with remarkable quiet on the gravel.

'There are some rather odd foot- or hoof-prints here and I think we should take casts of them,' Dawlish said. 'I also think there has been serious trouble and we need a team out here quickly as well as a doctor. I haven't looked round to see if any windows are open, but – '

'There's one open at the front, we could get to it from the roof of the porch,' Hennessy said, glancing upwards. 'But I don't understand why you're so sure – '

'I've an unfair advantage over you,' Dawlish said tersely. 'Will you get more men?' He stood back and looked up at the roof of the porch, his eyes fastening on a narrow ledge on the outside of the brickwork. 'If I haven't opened the door in five minutes send someone up after me.'

He moved towards the ledge.

To Felicity, his wife for over twenty years, he was a changed man, moving with a speed and speaking with an authority which he seldom showed in her presence. One moment he was standing by her side; the next he had a foot on the ledge and, one arm stretched as high

28

as it would go, a grip on the top of the porch. He hauled himself up with a movement so swift that it made the man with Hennessy exclaim:

'Look at *that*.'

Hennessy was staring upwards and at the same time taking his walkie-talkie from his breast pocket. He saw Dawlish standing at his full height as he, the Chief Inspector, began to give instructions to the Kingston Divisional Headquarters. Dawlish leaned forward towards an open window on the right, and pushed from the top; it was a sash-cord type window and opened smoothly to a gap of at least two feet.

Felicity saw him grip the top and then swing off the porch roof.

'Pat!' she gasped in a strangled voice.

'Shouldn't worry about *him*, ma'am,' said the detective sergeant. 'I had a physical training instructor once. That kind of thing's easy – if you know how to do it. See! He's in!'

Dawlish made an upward swing, dived through the window, and in a flash was out of sight. Hennessy, who had watched every movement while giving instructions, switched off his walkie-talkie and then said briskly:

'See if you can find another way in.'

'I could go the same way, sir.'

'Mr Dawlish may not want you to.'

Felicity was startled out of her mood of tension by that remark, for it proved that Hennessy was perceptive and somehow attuned to Dawlish. She felt hot as he moved from the porch to the car, and glanced towards the hoof-marks. The cloven hoof. Why had Pat been so affected? A pony, a tiny calf – she stopped thinking, she did not want to appear absurd even to herself.

29

A light went on in the room beyond the window where Dawlish had disappeared.

Dawlish stood by the doorway of what he could now see was a small dressing-room. It was approached by a wide passage in which, to the right, were three more doors, and to the left one door and a staircase with a half-landing. A dim light gleamed from the hall.

He heard a sound; it might have been a moan.

He stepped further into the passage and saw that the door next to the dressing-room was open. As he moved towards it he heard another sound and this time he had no doubt at all that it was a moan.

He went towards this door, seeing that the room beyond was in total darkness.

He reached it, as the moaning grew not louder but more constant; it was interspersed with a low, broken muttering.

'No, don't hurt me. Don't hurt me. No!' There was a muted scream. '*No!*'

Dawlish groped for and found the light switch, and four lights came on at the walls. He saw the large, luxuriously furnished room, the two beds and the near-naked woman lying on one of them.

She was rolling her head from side to side as the moaning came, and her lips moved with the words though her eyes remained tightly closed. He felt his own tension clamping every nerve in his body but broke its hold and went slowly towards the woman, saying in a quiet voice:

'It's all right now, Ursula. It's all right now.'

He did not think she heard him, certainly she gave no sign. He drew nearer. He could see the tiny marks where hypodermic syringes had been used to pump drugs into her. He could see a burn on her cheek. He could see the marks of cords which had bound her wrists and ankles. And he knew almost exactly what had happened to this woman.

Burnt on her body was a mark, sharp and clear.

It was the shape of a cloven hoof.

Moving very slowly, very gently, he picked up a sheet and draped it over her, but she did not seem to notice. Nothing stopped the subconscious movement of her head, from right to left, from left to right, as if in remembered agony.

'Devil!' she gasped, and then in a louder voice: '*Devil!*'

She tried to raise her head but did not have the strength, and now almost the only word which came from her lips was: *Devil*.

She opened her eyes.

She stared straight at Dawlish but obviously she did not see him. There was a mask of sheer terror on her face, terror in her eyes.

'Devil!' she gasped. 'Devil!'

Then her head dropped and her eyes closed and for the first time since Dawlish had come into the room she lay still and silent, as if some merciful oblivion had taken full hold of her and for a while she was not filled with these awful fears.

Dawlish turned away.

He felt very clammy at the back of the neck, and there was nausea in his stomach. He went to the door and as he reached it heard footsteps in the hall downstairs, Hennessy's voice, followed by that of a man whom Dawlish had not heard before. Another policeman? He stood at the landing railings, gripping the polished wood so tightly that it hurt his knuckles, and looked down. Hennessy was with a much older, white-haired man, certainly far too old to be a policeman. A doctor already?

'But what can possibly have happened? Where is Lady Franklin – ' The old man was looking upwards and, seeing Dawlish, backed away in alarm, hands raised as if to fend off some attack from high above his head. He had long, silvery hair and a pink face. 'There's a man up there!' he cried. 'There's a strange man!'

'It's all right, Mr Ranniker,' Hennessy soothed. 'Mr Dawlish is from – '

'Scotland Yard,' Dawlish called down. 'Chief Inspector, is the doctor on the way?'

'Yes, sir.'

'*Doctor!*' echoed Ranniker. 'Who needs a doctor? Not Lady Ursula, oh, please God, not Lady Ursula.' He moved towards the foot of the stairs, very quick for an old man and so agile that he was halfway up the stairs before Hennessy caught up with him. By then Dawlish was at the half-landing, a head taller than each of the other men. 'It can't be Lady Ursula, she can't be hurt – '

'Mr Ranniker,' Dawlish said as gently as he could. 'She has been hurt and will need a doctor at once – better get an ambulance,' he added over the old man's shoulder, then went on without a change of tone: 'I am in touch with Sir Justin, and I'm going to talk to him in a few minutes. Meanwhile – '

'If anything happens to her I'll kill myself,' Ranniker said in a hoarse voice. 'Sir Justin left me in charge, I should never have left the house, I wouldn't have but for the fact that my daughter – '

Brokenly, he told the story, which Hennessy's ser-

32

geant took down in shorthand; by the time he had
finished the old man appeared to be on the point of
collapse, breaking into sobs of distress, adding that Sir
Justin would never forgive him, nor would he ever forgive himself. If Lady Ursula were to die he would kill
himself.

'The one thing you have to get into your head is that
even if you had been here it would have made no difference,' Dawlish told him. 'The men who burgled this
house would either have murdered you or trussed you
up. In one way it's a very good job you and your wife
were not here. How far away does your daughter
live?'

'In Kingston, sir, but she – she's in the hospital. My
wife's at her home, though, with our son-in-law. He – '

'We'll have you taken there,' Dawlish promised.
'And remember what I have said: you could not possibly have prevented what happened. Lady Ursula is
alive and I've told you that I'm in touch with her husband. You go and get some rest.'

'Rest?' echoed the old man, bitterly. '*I'll* never rest
again after this.'

But he allowed himself to be led off by one of the
newcomers, who, it proved, was a friend of the Ranniker family. Dawlish watched him go out of the front
door while Hennessy stood by, his latest set of instructions already passed on by radio. The front door
closed, and Dawlish and Hennessy were the only two
left in the hall.

'Chief Inspector,' Dawlish said quietly, 'will you
have every part of Ranniker's story checked closely,
make sure there isn't the slightest discrepancy, not the
slightest possibility that he was lying.'

Hennessy opened his mouth as if to fling out questions, then said: 'Yes, sir. Right away. But – how is Lady Ursula?'

'I am afraid she is in a very bad way indeed,' Dawlish said. 'Get that done and then come upstairs, will you? Have the doctor come straight up as soon as he arrives. Oh – and have you seen that casts are taken of those footprints?'

'Yes,' Hennessy said. There was a peculiar expression in his eyes. 'The men making the casts *say* that they look like cloven hoofs,' he added, darting a quick look at Dawlish.

'They do,' Dawlish said.

4 *Frantic Husband*

The woman on the bed was quiet now, her agonized voice silent, yet it was possible to imagine an echo of her screaming hurled back from the walls and the doors, the huge built-in wardrobe which took up the whole of one wall, the glass of the great mirror over a long dressing-table where every imaginable kind of toilet accessory, creams and powders, lipsticks and rouge, lotions and mascara, lay: everything which was considered an aid to beauty. The colourings in the room were gold and a pale green; the sheet which Dawlish had spread over the unconscious woman matched the green of the eiderdown on the other bed, which had, apparently, not been touched. Dawlish moved to the telephone beside it and dialled for the operator.

When she answered he thought: I've forgotten Felicity.

He gave the Manchester number and held on, but Franklin answered so quickly that he must have been awake with his hand poised to snatch up the receiver.

'This is Franklin.'

'Justin,' Dawlish said quietly, 'you were quite right, there has been trouble.'

There was a moment's silence: then, little above a whisper, the words: 'Oh, dear God, dear God.' There was another moment of silence before he spoke again in a voice which was commendably steady. 'Is Ursula hurt?'

'She isn't in danger of dying,' Dawlish answered.

'She isn't – ' Franklin hesitated, seemed to gulp, and then demanded in a stronger voice: 'What are you saying?'

'I am saying that she has had a bad time, that she is unconscious and will soon be on the way to hospital, and there may be more positive news when you get here. And I'm saying that she isn't in danger of dying.'

Another silence followed before Franklin stated flatly: 'You're keeping something back.'

'Yes,' Dawlish said, 'because I can't tell you everything in five minutes and you won't be able to form any balanced judgement until you've heard it all.'

'Damn balanced judgement! You're talking about my wife.'

'If you go straight to the airport at Manchester and ask for the airport police I'll arrange for you to come to London by helicopter or a police aircraft,' Dawlish said. 'I'll try to make it a helicopter because then you can land on the Westminster helicopter landing stage, and you'll be near the Mandel Clinic where I'm going

35

to send Ursula. It's in Westminster, and a driver will be at the landing stage or wherever you land to take you there. And I'll be waiting.'

Again there was silence; and no doubt at all that Franklin would like to hurl a hundred urgent questions, but after the pause, he said:

'Thanks. One thing.'

'Yes?'

'What happened to the Rannikers?'

'Their daughter was suddenly taken ill, in childbirth, and Ursula told them they could go and see her,' Dawlish said. 'They're being looked after – but not at your house.'

'Why not?'

'I think we should have control of the house for a while,' Dawlish said, and added with a tone of finality: 'I will tell you the whole story and answer all your questions as soon as I possibly can.'

As he rang off, Dawlish heard footsteps cross the hall and mount the stairs. This would be Hennessy, but would the police surgeon be with him? He dialled his office number as Hennessy and a brisk-looking young man, with black jutting eyebrows and a pale face, hovered in the doorway. Dawlish put a finger to his lips and then heard the operator at his office: the man who had spoken to him before.

'Who is on night duty?' he asked.

'Chief Inspector Pence, sir.'

'Put him through,' Dawlish said, and then beckoned the other two in and said quietly: 'I won't be two minutes. Will you see if you can find any ampoules from hypodermic injection, or any evidence of electrical devices having been used here?' Both men were startled, but both were kept busy while Dawlish spoke to the man who was in charge of the office and administrative side of the Department's affairs. Pence never needed telling anything twice, although he seldom took notes.

'I'll arrange all that, sir. Will they be expecting a patient at the Mandel Clinic?'

'I knew I'd forgot something! No,' said Dawlish, 'but you'll fix it with them and if there is any difficulty at all telephone Dr Mandel at his home and tell him what I've asked for.'

'Very good, sir.' Pence rang off, while the dark-haired man with the pale face stood up from an examination of the floor on the far side of the bed, looked across at Dawlish almost accusingly, and then asked abruptly:

'Did you mention Dr Mandel of the Mandel Clinic?'

'Yes.'

'But he specializes in neuro-surgery and brain damage.'

'Yes,' Dawlish said. 'I know. Are you Dr – '

'Smith,' supplied Hennessy, and added: 'Sorry.'

'I hope you won't think I've usurped your authority,' Dawlish said to Smith with a pleasant smile, 'but I think the Mandel Clinic is the one place which might help. You see,' he said without a change of tone or expression and yet with a bleakness which seemed to make the room go cold, 'I think Lady Franklin has been the victim of a deliberate attempt to drive her insane. I don't know whether there is any brain damage, I do know that she must have undergone an ordeal which in itself would be enough to turn the minds of many people.' He paused long enough to let his glance rest on the lovely face with the red and angry burn scar on the left cheek. 'Why don't you examine her, Dr Smith?'

37

Slowly, as if he were made reluctant by what Dawlish had said, the police surgeon began to turn back the sheet. Suddenly, he caught his breath, at sight of the burn scars and of the tiny incisions, the puncture marks of the hypodermic needle – and, at last, the brand of the cloven hoof.

The mark was much more vivid, now, and in its outline quite unmistakable; it was identical, though smaller, with those found in the flower-bed beneath this very room.

'What the devil is going on?' demanded Smith in a taut voice. 'What do you know of this, Mr Dawlish?'

'Both too much and too little,' Dawlish answered.

'Are you implying that this kind of thing has happened before?'

'I am stating it,' Dawlish said.

'You mean –' Hennessy's voice and expression showed that he was more shaken by this remark than by anything that had been said before, and he had lost every vestige of colour; he looked a very plain man. 'You mean, abroad?'

'Here and overseas, yes,' Dawlish said, and he put a hand on Hennessy's forearm. 'You don't need telling that this is extremely confidential, do you?'

'I – I shall have to put it in my report.'

'Only to your superintendent, please, in your handwriting if needs be. No typist and no photographer should see it.'

'I – I type,' Hennessy said.

Smith, having looked from one man to the other with apparent suspicion, was now making a closer examination of some of the marks. Dawlish and Hennessy moved to the other side of the room. The sergeant who had been here from the beginning was coming up the stairs; he was a boyish-looking, fresh-faced man with a shock of hair which seemed to rise straight up from his forehead, an effect heightened by the fact that it was clipped very short at the sides.

Dawlish went to the door.

'I have a message from your office, sir. Everything has been arranged at Mandel's clinic.'

'Good.'

'Er – may I ask what about your wife, sir?'

'I'll come down and see her,' Dawlish promised, and turned to Hennessy. 'I'd wait a while before you go over this room – do you think your Chief Constable would be willing to consult the Yard?'

'I'm positive, sir.'

'Then have him ask for Superintendent Naismith.'

'I will,' Hennessy promised. 'I'll call him right away.'

Obviously Hennessy was quite sure that his Chief Constable would not object to being woken in the small hours, equally sure that his man was predictable. He, Dawlish, went downstairs on the heels of the sergeant. Three plain-clothes men were checking the floor, as if for more prints, and when he got outside he saw that a rope had been made into a kind of fence round the flower-beds, and the imprints of the cloven hoofs were now filled with plaster of paris which showed up very white. He crossed to his car where Felicity was sitting in the seat next to the driver's, and she watched him closely as he got in, saying over his shoulder:

'Thank you, Sergeant.'

'Pleasure, sir.' The sergeant smoothed down his up-standing hair as he backed away. Dawlish looked at Felicity, groped for and found her hand, then sat back with his eyes closed. He did not speak for some time and she did not move. In the distance an ambulance bell rang.

He said quickly: 'She is not dead.'

'I'm glad,' replied Felicity.

'I'm not sure that you should be,' Dawlish said, and at last he turned his head and looked at her. 'It is very, very nasty.'

'Can you tell me?'

'Not yet. What have you heard?'

'There's been a lot of talk of cloven hoofs.'

'And of devil worship?'

'*Pat!*'

'It always follows,' Dawlish said bitterly. 'Or nearly always.'

'Pat,' Felicity said in a sharper voice, 'must you be so mysterious?'

'Not intentionally mysterious,' he replied, 'just inescapably obscure. I'm sorry, my darling. Had I dreamt that this was going to happen I wouldn't have brought you along. I can't talk about it yet, it's – well, let's say it's *sub judice*. Ursula Franklin, who is a very beautiful young woman, has been cruelly tortured. I have to meet her husband in I suppose an hour's time. The woman will be taken away in the ambulance and then we can go. It might be another half-hour. I could send you back, I'm sure Chief Inspector Hennessy would supply a car.'

'I'll stay,' she said.

'Would you like to go into the house?' asked Dawlish. 'It's warmer.'

Felicity looked past him to the house and slowly shook her head.

'I'd rather stay out here,' she said.

As she spoke, an ambulance turned into the carriage-

40

way. Dawlish nodded understandingly as he got out of the car and walked to the house.

Before he disappeared she saw him glance towards the plaster in the hoof-prints, and she shivered.

Once within the house, Dawlish became aware of an atmosphere which could not be mistaken. All the men were on edge, much more than one would expect at a straightforward murder investigation. How much of the atmosphere was due to what had happened to Ursula Franklin? And how much to the talk and the evidence of the cloven hoof?

The devil's footprints.

He saw ambulance men in the bedroom with Dr Smith supervising the moving of the unconscious woman, now wrapped in a sheet. Hennessy, in the corridor outside the room, moved across to Dawlish.

'Everything Ranniker says has been checked and corroborated, sir. His daughter is still on the danger list. Something went wrong with the breech birth.'

Dawlish nodded.

'Right. The next thing is – who was likely to know that Lady Franklin would be alone?'

'I'll do what I can,' promised Hennessy. 'And I've talked to the Chief Constable who is sending at once for Yard help and specifying Superintendent Naismith.'

'Good,' Dawlish said, and then very warmly: 'Chief Inspector, you've been splendid. I couldn't have had better co-operation.'

'Nice of you,' Hennessy mumbled, and actually seemed to blush. 'I'll keep right on this job, sir.'

'I'm sure you will.' Dawlish stood back as the ambulance men carried the woman out, and then went downstairs, explaining that he would see Franklin in London.

'Better you than me, sir,' Hennessy said frankly. 'Those cloven hoof-prints – *can* they mean anything?'

'Oh, they mean something,' Dawlish assured him, but did not elaborate. 'I'll be off, Chief Inspector. Again – warm thanks.' The power of his hand-grip nearly crushed Hennessy's fingers.

When he reached the car Felicity had moved to the steering wheel, and he became a willing passenger. There was little traffic, and after five minutes they sped past the ambulance. Neither made any comment. The journey took only twenty-five minutes. As Felicity pulled in towards the entrance of the building where they had their penthouse, a Yard man moved towards them.

'Sir Justin Franklin will be at the Westminster Bridge landing stage in about fifteen minutes, sir.'

'Ah,' said Dawlish. 'Thanks.' He looked at Felicity, who was staring straight in front of her, and went on gently: 'It's not worth my coming in, darling. Up to you whether you wait to see Franklin, but it would be a boon if you'd make sure the spare room's ready.' He gripped her hand, and then as she got out, eased over to the driving seat. He was moving off by the time she reached the foyer, and he had not been at the helicopter station by Westminster Bridge five minutes, before he heard the unmistakable beat of a helicopter engine.

This would almost certainly be Franklin.

What should he say? How could he tell any man that such things had happened to a beloved wife?

5   Why?

Franklin was opening the sliding door in the bulbous nose of the helicopter before it landed on the wooden planks which made the platform. Lights from the bridge and the embankment shimmered on the smooth surface of the Thames; so did the reflection of the stars. The engine cut off and died away as Franklin jumped out, a tall man, lean and muscular but nothing like the size of Dawlish. The helicopter pilot climbed out, while men on duty at the landing stage watched Dawlish. Men from his own department also watched both from the embankment and the bridge.

Dawlish moved towards Franklin. There was enough light for each to see and recognize one another.

They did not shake hands as Franklin demanded: 'How is she?'

'Not well, Justin.'

'I don't want any more bloody mystery. I want to know what happened, here and now,' Franklin said. He gripped Dawlish's forearm and his fingers were like steel talons. 'No half-truths, no holds barred. What happened?'

The breeze off the river struck chill as Dawlish said quietly, almost mechanically:

'She was alone in the house because the servants had a family emergency. She was attacked by a number of men, I would say at least six. She was not raped. She was caused a great deal of pain – tortured. I haven't yet seen the medical report but I know of other cases where much the same thing has happened: in each case the torture has been by injection into certain veins and nerves; by electrolosis applied to spots of great sensitivity; by minor but extremely painful burns and incisions.'

He stopped.

All the time Franklin stood staring at him; and all the time Franklin's grip on his arm tightened until it became extremely painful, but Dawlish did nothing to ease it. By a trick of the light Franklin's eyes seemed to shimmer a silver colour; his breathing was harsh and discordant. When he spoke the words were difficult to understand.

'Is there more?'

'There were indications that powerful electric current was passed through her brain, where it is at least possible that the worst injury was done. Physically she will be recovered in a week. If she had only the recollection of what happened to recover from, it would be bad enough, for the ordeal by itself might be enough to derange some people, but there could be – and I think there is – damage to the brain by the electrical current and the injections. She needs the most skilled care and will need it for weeks, probably much longer. The man most competent to tell you about that is Dr Pierre Mandel, but I doubt if he can or will give any opinion until the morning.'

Dawlish stopped.

It was as if the breeze, stiffening now, had turned the other man into stone. Dawlish himself shivered; not only with the cold but with the possibility that he had been too blunt: harsh. Franklin had demanded the truth, but should he have softened the blow? To a certain extent he had done this. He had omitted details which could fill anyone with horror. But he

44

could have hedged. But there again the schoolboy he had known, and the man whose reputation he now recalled, would not have wanted compromise. Master Relativity, they had called him: the collector of cold facts.

There was another point: sooner or later Franklin would have to know everything; in one way it was better that he should know most of it now.

At last, he stirred, and asked very simply: 'But why?'

Dawlish said: 'I wish I knew.'

'You say you've met some similar devilry before. What was the motive?'

'A hundred of the top policemen in the world would give a great deal to know,' Dawlish told him. 'But – '

'You can't be serious.'

'I am desperately serious,' Dawlish assured him.

'I must see her.'

'They may not let you.'

Franklin growled: 'They'll let me. Unless – ' He caught his breath. 'They haven't disfigured her, have they?'

'No.'

'I must see her,' Franklin repeated.

'I'll drive you,' said Dawlish, and when they were both in the car, watched by all the policemen on duty, Franklin sat back and closed his eyes. Dawlish did not talk: now there was a brief period for adjustment and Franklin needed it very badly.

The clinic was between Harley and Wimpole Streets, and the drive took them less than ten minutes. As they pulled up just beyond the lighted sign at the front door, Franklin said in a jerky voice:

'Sorry if I'm boorish. Thanks.'

'Forget it.' They got out and as they approached the closed door with light which shone through frosted-glass panels, Dawlish went on: 'Do you know this place?'

'No. I've heard of it. One of the directors of a company I was working for went crazy and – ' Franklin broke off and drew in a deep, hissing breath. He looked as if there were unspeakable things on his mind.

'I know it fairly well,' Dawlish said, ignoring the other. 'If Mandel's here himself we'll have no trouble, if his chief assistant is here on duty he will make all kinds of difficulty.' He pressed a bell-push, and it was only a moment before footsteps sounded and a shadow appeared on the glass panels. The door was opened by a middle-aged, severe yet attractive-looking woman in nurse's uniform. The moment she saw Dawlish she stood aside.

'Good morning, Mr Dawlish.'

'Hallo, Mrs Bell.' As she closed the door, he went on: 'Justin, Mrs Bell is the senior nurse on duty at night – Sir Justin Franklin.'

'Is my wife here?' Franklin demanded harshly.

'Yes, Sir Justin,' she said. 'Dr Mandel himself is with her now.'

'I want to see her.'

'If you will come with me, I won't keep you long,' she promised.

She led the way upstairs. Once on the landing, it was apparent that several houses had been knocked into one, to make the clinic. The door of a small well-lit waiting-room was open. There were big, comfortable chairs, up-to-date magazines, two telephones and a sign on the table reading: 'No smoking, please'. Dawlish dropped into a chair, but Franklin began to pace up

46

and down. This was the first real opportunity Dawlish had had to study him, and his first reaction was how much older the man looked.

The lines in a striking face were now deeply etched, the chiselled features and well-shaped mouth cut more sharply. Suddenly he turned and faced Dawlish.

'How long will they be?'

'Not a moment longer than they can help.'

'Why shouldn't they let me go straight in?'

'Dr Mandel may be at a delicate stage in his preliminary examination.'

Franklin glared. Dawlish could wish that the numbed state of shock would last longer. Feeling would be so much more painful.

'Is he the best man available?'

'I think so.'

'Thinking isn't good enough.'

'Leading doctors and surgeons who specialize in brain disorders throughout the world consult him and send patients to him. I don't think there is a better man.'

Franklin said: 'If there is, I want him.'

Dawlish did not speak. There was a limit to how a man, even one so distraught, should talk, and in Franklin there was a hectoring note, the rasp of a man who always got his own way. It would not be good for him to think that he could ride roughshod over Dr Mandel, or for that matter over Dawlish. Perhaps all this showed in Dawlish's eyes, for suddenly Franklin relaxed and dropped into a chair.

'I – I am sorry, Dawlish. I feel as if I'm in hell.'

'Everyone here, everyone you meet among the police, is going to do everything possible to help,' Dawlish assured him.

47

'And they won't help so much if I throw my weight about?'

'Some might not,' conceded Dawlish.

The door opened without warning and Franklin sprang to his feet as a man appeared, a stocky man with broad shoulders and a short neck. He wore a knee-length white smock over a pair of pyjamas. Pince-nez looked out of place and almost absurd on the broad face, stamped indelibly with authority. He glanced at, but did not speak to, Dawlish, addressing Franklin.

'Sir Justin, your wife is sleeping, and I want her to sleep undisturbed for at least twelve hours. If you wish you may see her through a glass screen, but you must not enter her room.'

'If I can just see her – ' Franklin's voice broke.

'Then come with me. Join us if you wish, Mr Dawlish.'

Dawlish thought: This isn't the moment, and Mandel will tell me anything worth knowing afterwards. 'No, thank you,' he murmured. Mandel nodded briefly, as if in approval, and followed Franklin who was already outside the waiting-room. Once the door closed Dawlish half-wished he had gone along, and then returned to his first decision: this was better, this was a moment which Franklin would not want to share. He sat down again and picked up a copy of *Country Life*, but nothing interested him and there was only one question in his mind: *Why?*

Ursula lay still.

The sheets were drawn up beneath her chin and the burn mark showed up vividly on her cheek. She might have been asleep – or dead. The room beyond the big window was like any small hospital ward, and everything was white. Her husband's breathing became laboured as he at last turned to Mandel.

'She is alive, isn't she?' he asked hoarsely.

'She is in no danger of dying.'

'She *will* get better, won't she?'

'If human knowledge and skill can make her better – yes.'

'You sound as if she might not!'

'Sir Justin, it is not pleasant to have to tell you that your wife is gravely ill, that there is some evidence of damage to the nerve system and the brain cells, and that there is also absolutely no way, at this stage, of being sure whether the damage can be repaired. I hope very much that it can. I have known cases which on first examination appear to be far worse than your wife recover completely. But I would be lying if I told you that recovery can be guaranteed.'

Franklin drew in a searing breath, and his tormented eyes seemed to foreshadow the question which came out almost with a stammer as he fought to maintain self-control.

'But – but – *why*? Why should anyone do this to my wife? Why – '

'If anyone at any time can answer that question I believe it is Mr Dawlish,' replied Mandel. 'Shall we go and join him?' He put a hand at Franklin's elbow and led him away.

Franklin turned blindly once again; but he could see nothing but the white wall.

Dawlish heard the sound of men approaching, and was on his feet. Mandel ushered Franklin into the room, and Dawlish, seeing the anguish on the man's

49

face, could understand something of the torment.

'I will be in touch with you as soon as possible in the morning, Mr Dawlish,' Mandel said.

'Thank you. In general, are the indications the same as we've seen before?'

'In general, yes,' replied Mandel.

With a murmured 'Good night' he turned and went out, while Franklin stood fighting back tears, fighting back a complete loss of control. Dawlish gave him three or four minutes and then said in a matter-of-fact voice: 'Let's go, Justin.' The other man did not even ask where, but turned and followed him blindly, along the passage, down the stairs and out into the street. No one was in sight. Dawlish opened the passenger door and Franklin got in mechanically. Next he went round to the driving side and got in. He was very, very tired, he wished in a way that he had a driver. He could send for one. He actually hesitated, then shrugged, started the engine, and switched on the lights.

As he did so, his heart seemed to turn over and then began to thump against his ribs. For a few seconds he just sat, staring at the apparition caught in the head-lamp beams.

Only – it could not be an apparition; this was a man-made picture.

It was fastened to the back of the car in front of Dawlish's, the face of Mephistopheles, painted in phosphorescent paint which added an unearthly glow to the eyes, to the familiar, pointed features, the horns growing out of the forehead.

The whole thing seemed to be smouldering – and suddenly it burst into flames.

6 Another Victim

Until the moment when the Mephistophelean head burst into flames Dawlish did not know whether Franklin, deep in misery, had seen it. Now it was a mass of leaping flames with the face still so far unscathed, tongues of fire writhing from the eyes and also from the mouth. Dawlish felt the other man stir and lean forward, muttering:

'What the hell is that?'

'It seems that someone's thought up a nice line in fireworks.'

'Fireworks? Why, that – that's the face of the devil!'

'It's a devilish face, certainly,' Dawlish agreed.

The flames were beginning to die down. A car slowed down behind them and stopped alongside. A man came running along the pavement, visible in Dawlish's side mirror: it was a policeman. A window went up across the street and a man bellowed in a shrill voice: 'Fire, fire!' The policeman called across to the alarmist:

'All safe now, sir.'

'But there's a fire!'

'It's nearly out, sir.'

A young man got out of the car rather gingerly. Dawlish joined him and the policeman. All three gathered at a respectful distance, and the young man said in a voice both nervous and hopeful: 'It won't blow up, will it?'

Dawlish shook his head. Nothing that had happened in this affair suggested that the people behind it meant to kill.

'We could call the fire department,' he suggested.

'I have, sir,' replied the policeman. 'When I saw it from the end of the street it looked as if a car was on fire, and if that had been so the petrol tank *would* have blown up.' He drew a little nearer. 'It's a metal contraption fastened on to the rear bumper. The mask is metal, too.' The light from his torch seemed to grow more powerful as the embers died.

A police car drew up, and very soon afterwards a fire-engine. People had gathered, too, some from nearby houses, some passers-by. The charred ruin of the apparition was so shapeless that none of the newcomers could make out the definition of the face.

The constable who had been the first to arrive asked: 'You saw it all, sir, didn't you? If you would tell me – '

Dawlish took a card from his pocket and as the constable flashed his torch on the letters, said quietly: 'I think it was intended to scare me and the gentleman with me. We need to find out who secured it to the car – it wasn't there when we arrived about three-quarters of an hour ago. I must leave that to you chaps.'

'I'm sorry, sir – ' the constable began, and then he exclaimed: 'Mr *Dawlish*. The Deputy AC!'

'Did I show you one of my private cards?' Dawlish saw that he had. 'That shows you how tired I must be. I'll have a full statement ready in the morning.' He turned back to the car, eyed curiously by two or three of the people nearby. He looked among them for anyone who might appear even remotely as if he had been involved in the 'joke', but saw no one.

Franklin hadn't moved from his seat.

'We'll go to my place, it's not far,' Dawlish said. 'You're welcome to the spare room.'

52

The other man made no comment, and soon they were turning towards Wigmore Street. The lights gave the whole area a deserted appearance, as if this were a city of the dead.

Franklin sat unmoving and unspeaking.

Dawlish pulled into the driveway of the building at Millbank. One of his own men was on duty there but apart from a 'Good night, sir' had nothing to say; so there was no kind of emergency. There was another man, also from Dawlish's section of the Criminal Investigation Department, in the dimly lit foyer. 'Good night, sir.' 'Good night.' Dawlish stood aside as the man pressed for the lift; the doors opened immediately and he stepped inside, Franklin moving mechanically beside him. Shock? That wouldn't be surprising, and if so he needed a sedative: Dawlish could give him one by injection or by pill, once they were upstairs. The lift came to a gentle halt, and Dawlish stepped out – and again his heart seemed to turn over.

A man stood opposite the doorway.

For a single moment fear flared up in Dawlish, but then it died, for this was Gordon Scott, second-in-command of the Department. When he saw that he had startled Dawlish he said:

'Sorry, sir. Didn't want to worry Mrs Dawlish, but I needed a word with you.'

'Ah,' Dawlish said. 'That can only mean trouble.'

'In a way I'm afraid that is so, sir.' Gordon, a man in his middle thirties, fresh-complexioned, with sandy-coloured hair and freckles, looked at Franklin, who appeared to take no interest at all in what was going on. 'A – ah – another case was found tonight.'

Dawlish drew in a harsh breath, then said evenly: 'Go on.'

'She was found by a neighbour.' With brief economy of words, Gordon Scott reported the finding of the older woman near Epping, making it clear that the sign of the cloven hoof had been discovered near the house where the woman had been attacked. 'We're getting everything we can about her, sir, there'll be a full report in the morning, but I wondered if you would like to send her to Dr Mandel.'

Dawlish said: 'I'll talk to him.'

He actually had to guide Franklin by the arm as he unlocked the door and entered the flat. On the instant he stopped, for another door across the passage was open and he could see Felicity lying on a couch, her shoes on the floor, her face turned towards the wall. She was fast asleep. She didn't stir as Dawlish quietly closed the door and then led Franklin along the passage to the spare bedroom, Scott hovering behind them.

When that was done Dawlish dialled Mandel's number on a telephone on the kitchen bar. Mrs Bell answered.

'Yes, he is still awake, I'll put you through,' she said, and a moment later Mandel himself came on the line.

Dawlish told him what he had learned.

'Yes, I understand,' Mandel said, in an exhausted voice, 'and you are quite right, the sooner I see her the more easy it will be to find out if the same techniques and possibly the same instruments were used. Was there the branding of the cloven hoof?'

'Yes.'

'If she is at Epping it will be an hour before she can be brought here, so I shall get a little sleep,' Mandel said, as if he were smothering a yawn. 'I will

54

endeavour to have reports on both victims tomorrow.'

'Thank you,' Dawlish said. 'May I ask one question?'

'If you must.'

'What was your impression of Sir Justin Franklin's reaction?'

'My impression of Sir Justin is that he has for a long time been living on his nerves. Many highly skilled and exceptional men of similar calibre come to me because, by driving themselves as hard as they do, they create lapses in memory and concentration, even sometimes to the point of hallucinations. You will, of course, give him a strong sedative. Pettatol, if you have a supply, preferably by injection.'

'I can do that,' Dawlish said.

'I can also tell you that he could be in a very serious condition and that the shock of what happened tonight might make him seriously ill. If he does not show positive signs of normality within twelve hours I think I should see him – or at least that he should see some other person equally qualified.'

'Is there anyone?' asked Dawlish drily.

'Oh, many, for his condition,' Mandel replied. 'Good night.'

Dawlish hesitated before putting down the receiver. He glanced at his watch, surprised to see that it was only ten minutes past three, not really as late as he expected. He went along to the spare room, where Scott stood alone; but the door of the bathroom which led off was open and Dawlish could hear taps running.

'Bring the other woman to London and take her straight to the clinic,' Dawlish ordered.

Scott's face brightened. 'Good!' Then the brightness and the youthfulness seemed to vanish and he went on: 'What the hell *is* going on, sir? This must be the fifth

55

in England and the lord knows how many throughout the world.'

After a long pause Dawlish said with great precision: 'Exactly one hundred and seven, unless there have been more reports since I left the office.' He saw the shock register on Gordon Scott's face, and realized that in one way at least this was the first time the true gravity and the horror of the situation had affected him. There *were* sadists: devils, it seemed, in human form, who would perform acts of unbelievable cruelty for their own pleasure. No policeman would ever be surprised at what a man would do to a man, to a woman or even to a child. Each was an isolated act in itself, but when such crimes were organized and carried out on, and by, numbers, it was a different matter.

What was happening now was part of a pattern, and the picture was not only in England but in a dozen countries abroad.

Scott stared for what seemed a long time into the bleak face of his chief, then turned and went out: he would call the Epping Police from his car and set things in motion. Now he, Dawlish, had to deal only with Justin Franklin, and he was by no means certain that Franklin would submit to an injection.

Footsteps sounded, and Franklin pushed open the door and stepped in. He still looked very tired, but gave the impression of being more in control of himself. His voice, when he spoke, was even and unemotional.

'I am not myself and won't be until my wife has recovered. But I'm sufficiently myself to want to help put the men who tortured her in – in jail. I intend to drop everything so as to do that. If I can I'll work

56

with you. I mean, of course, if you will let me. If you won't I'll find a way of working against them on my own.'

Dawlish said, slowly: 'I hate making conditions.'

'What conditions?'

'I've a sedative here which I'd like to give you – in the form of a shot. It will take much of the pressure off you and enable you to relax and think more clearly and act less emotionally.'

'Less emotionally! My God, what do you think I am? A bloodless robot?'

'I think you're a human being in a state of shock, and that you hate these people so much that at the moment all you can think of is killing them. I can't – no policeman could – use a man in such a condition. But if the effect of this shot is what I – and Dr Mandel – think it will be, you should be much more rational tomorrow.'

'And then you would let me help?'

'Then, as now, I want your help,' Dawlish said.

Franklin stared at him for what seemed a long time and then said quietly: 'I'll do it your way. I must admit I could do with something to put me out for a few hours.' He gave a mirthless grin. 'The return of sanity, you see.' The word was hardly out of his mouth before his face was contorted as if with pain, and in a taut voice he went on: 'What a damnable thing to say.'

Dawlish said: 'What a natural thing to say. Will you have some tea or coffee, a sandwich, or – '

'Coffee, please.'

'Good.' Dawlish led the way out of this room and along to the kitchen. There was still no sign of Felicity, and he plugged in a kettle and put out biscuits, butter

57

and cheese. 'Is there anyone you would like me to
tell?' he asked.

'Like whom?'

'Near relations?'

'My wife has no parents.'

'Oh,' Dawlish said, lamely. 'I'm sorry.'

'They died a long time ago, too long to get senti-
mental,' replied Franklin. 'You could have my office
telephoned and my appointments cancelled for the next
few days, including one with the Finance Committee
of the Manchester City Council.'

'I will do that. White or black?'

'White, please. No sugar.'

The kettle was already boiling and Dawlish made
the coffee and then pushed the cheese board and a tray
towards Franklin, who hesitated, then took a biscuit
and buttered it. Dawlish sat on a high bar stool,
Franklin in Felicity's kitchen armchair.

'*Was* that the face of the devil?' demanded Franklin.

'It was a mask made to look like the popular con-
ception of Mephistopheles, yes,' Dawlish said. 'A very
impressive firework.'

'At the time I hardly knew what it was, but I'm
beginning to see a lot of things which didn't register
before. *Did* your man tell you that another woman
had suffered in the same way tonight?'

'Yes.'

'Who?'

'I don't yet know.'

'You keep bloody calm about it!'

'I have to keep calm,' Dawlish retorted. 'I'm working against it.'

'There have been others?'

58

'In several parts of the world,' Dawlish answered.

'And you don't know why?'

'Not yet.'

'Who else knows about it?'

'All the police forces which have delegates to the World Convention of Policemen,' Dawlish answered, 'and yes, all of them have been working on it, without success. But I'd rather tell you more about this tomorrow,' he added, and stifled a vast yawn. 'I need some sleep, and you – '

'Perhaps I'd better have my shot,' Franklin said drily.

Dawlish had a fuller idea of the power of the man, and could not fail to admire the strength with which he had fought his way out of the effect of the shock.

'Was that the first time you'd seen Mephistopheles?'

Slowly, Dawlish shook his head.

'No. It goes with every one of the crimes.'

'What do you think it means?' asked Franklin, but before Dawlish had time to reply he went on: 'Are you suggesting that someone is trying to imply that it's the work of the devil?'

Dawlish shrugged. 'If there is a devil, this is what one could expect from him.'

'You don't *believe* in the devil, do you?'

'Justin,' Dawlish said, 'I don't believe in ghosts, but I don't disbelieve in them, either. I believe in evil and cruelty and wicked men, and I believe in goodness and kindness and good men. I don't know whether whatever is happening here is through human agencies, but I would take a hell of a lot of convincing that there was anything supernatural behind it. I know it's going to take all I've got, and probably all you've got, and the efforts of a lot of powerful and experienced

59

policemen, before the truth is discovered. Now! How about that shot?'

'I'll just finish my coffee,' Franklin said, and drank with slow deliberation.

The expression in his eyes gave Dawlish more than a twinge of uneasiness, but he put it down to his own mood, and the shock upon shock which had come this night.

'When you're in bed I'll come and give it to you,' he said, and went out of the room.

The night was full of problems, still. Should he wake Felicity or leave her on the couch where she might sleep soundly until morning? How right was he to feel nervous about Justin Franklin? Both were mere trifles compared with the question: why had that burning mask been used? To frighten him? No one had attempted to do that before. He peeped in at Felicity, who hadn't stirred, and decided to leave her, went into their bedroom, changed into pyjamas in record time, unlocked the special drawer in the bedroom where he kept drugs, syringes, a variety of things which he might need in the course of duty but which few knew he possessed. He took out one of the latest plastic hypodermic syringes and pierced the top of an ampoule of Pettatol, and, with the syringe loaded, went along to the spare bedroom.

Justin Franklin wasn't there.

7 The Vanishing Man

Dawlish felt quite sure that Franklin had run away, but before he checked with the men on duty downstairs he searched the apartment and found no trace of the man; no wonder the expression in those pale eyes had made him uneasy. He called down to the foyer and asked the man who answered:

'Did you see which way Sir Justin Franklin went?'

'The man who came in with you, sir? Yes, he turned towards Parliament Square, and picked up a taxi.'

'Thanks,' Dawlish said gruffly. 'Good night.'

He rang off.

He was at once exasperated with himself and angry with Franklin, but he did not think he should put a call out for the man. If he were needed for any kind of questioning he could soon be found, for he was not likely to stay away from Mandel's clinic very long. Dawlish went back to bed. He wasn't sure he was right to leave Felicity but he was sure that he was dropping on his feet. So he pulled the bedclothes over him, switched off the bedside light, and turned on his side.

It could not have been more than five minutes later when he felt a hand at his shoulder. Half-dead with fatigue, he willed it away. But the hand stayed. Moreover, it shook his shoulder with great insistence.

'Pat,' said Felicity's voice, 'you must wake up.'

'Impossible,' he said, and had seldom meant anything more.

'You *must*. Dr Mandel wants you to call him.'

Dawlish forced one eye to open and perceived Felicity fully dressed in something brown and pink, and declared:

'Call him later.'

'He says it's very urgent.'

'Dammit,' protested Dawlish, 'I can't even have forty winks.'

'It's half past eleven – in the morning.'

Dawlish, startled, opened the other eye. Felicity had a beauty all her own. She looked fresh and wholesome and desirable.

'Come to bed,' he suggested.

'Idiot. *Do* you want your morning tea or don't you?'

'No. Give it to Dr Mandel.'

'Pat,' Felicity said in a different, a despairing tone of voice, 'don't play the fool, *please*. Dr Mandel telephoned and said he wanted to discuss a matter of the gravest importance with you.'

Dawlish's whole body went still.

Until that moment he had been vaguely aware of what had happened last night, but his mind had been only half-functioning. Now Felicity's tone brought full awareness. He eased himself up in bed and hitched a pillow behind him, and when Felicity moved forward to tuck another into position he slid his arm round her waist and hugged her. Then she drew back and pulled up a chair. He glanced at the bedside table to see tea and coffee there.

'Tea is becoming an hourly pleasure,' he said.

'I'm having coffee.'

'Is it half past eleven?'

'Well, it's twenty past.' Felicity poured out, and he balanced a cup and saucer in his left hand. 'What time did you get to bed?'

'About five, I suppose.'

'So Franklin didn't stay.'

' "Stay" is the word,' Dawlish said. 'He came, he saw, he fled – and he didn't get a glimpse of you on the couch so that could have been the explanation.' Gradually all the events of the night were coming clearly, most of them vividly, to his mind, and in a few minutes he would be ready to talk to Mandel. He wondered if he should call his office, first, and asked:

'Anything from Penny or Gordon Scott?'

'There have been three messages – will you call?'

'And you think Mandel should come first?'

'Pat,' said Felicity, 'you know what a calm man he is and he sounded terribly distressed. I really think you should call him. Here's his number.' She took a slip of paper from the tray, and shifted the telephone nearer so that he could dial more easily. He put his cup and saucer down, glanced at the number which he half-remembered, dialled, and waited; it seemed a long time before a woman answered:

'Dr Mandel's clinic, can I help you?'

'My name is Dawlish. I – '

Alarm seemed to flare up in the other's voice: 'Just a moment, Mr Dawlish. Dr Mandel has been trying to get you all the morning.'

That was the moment when the probable truth struck home to Dawlish and brought with it a great wave of depression. His fingers tightened about the receiver, and he looked away from the telephone so that Felicity should not see the expression in his eyes. Ursula had died, of course; the unexpected had happened, and Mandel had been wrong.

There were sounds on the telephone, then a sharper noise, then at last Pierre Mandel's voice.

63

'Mr Dawlish.'

'I'm sorry you've had so much trouble finding me,' Dawlish said.

'That is not trouble,' replied Mandel, and there was a break in his voice, the kind of catch which told how difficult he found it to pass on such news. 'Lady Franklin,' he said in a tone of disbelief. 'She has gone. Vanished. Disappeared. In the early hours of the morning someone came and took her away. I was not told until I woke an hour ago. Mr Dawlish! Someone came here and took Lady Franklin away. And I think this is the only place in the world where there is some hope of helping her to return to normal. Do you understand me? She has vanished!'

'I understand you perfectly,' Dawlish said. Hovering in his mind's eye was a vision of Justin's face, and the expression in his eyes when he had fooled Dawlish into thinking that he would take the shot without giving any trouble. That was when he had decided what to do: to take Ursula away.

'And the husband,' went on Mandel as if frantic, 'I do not care to think of the effect that this will have on him. But he is not a man from whom one should keep a secret. Dawlish – what am I to do?'

'For the moment, nothing,' Dawlish said. 'How many of your staff know about this?'

Perhaps three or four.'

'Can you rely on them to keep silent about it?'

'Absolutely,' Mandel assured him.

'Do any newspapers know?'

'*Mon Dieu*, why should I tell the newspapers?'

'Newspapermen have remarkable noses for sniffing out news,' Dawlish told him, 'and by now some of them are sure to have heard of the trouble at Esher last night and may have reasoned or discovered that Lady Franklin was brought to you. If anyone asks, deny it.'

'But of course.' There was a pause before Mandel went on: 'You mean we are to pretend that she did not come here?'

'For the time being, yes,' Dawlish replied. 'You've told me, so the police officially know. And I will keep in touch.' He was about to ring off when he raised his voice and exclaimed: 'Are you still there?'

'Yes, I am here,' Mandel said, as if a long way from the telephone.

'Did you have a chance to examine the other patient last night?'

'Oh, yes,' replied Mandel, and he added bitterly: 'I can also tell you that she is still here. She suffered similar wounds and similar injections, and I think she was the victim of people who used exactly the same techniques as those who attacked Lady Franklin.'

'But not the same individuals?'

'No, Mr Dawlish,' Mandel replied. 'The condition of this woman's brand is identical to the condition of that of Lady Franklin, and after careful examination I am quite certain that both scars were caused at the same time – yet one woman lives in Epping, the other in Esher. There are other indications, also. The angle at which the needles were inserted, and one or two bruises at the point of injection. All of these things convince me that a different man was involved.'

'Say nothing about any of this to anyone,' said Dawlish, 'and don't be surprised to find the clinic closely watched. I'll try to make surveillance as unobtrusive as I can but it will have to be thorough.'

'I fully understand,' Mandel told him.

Both men rang off at the same moment. Dawlish

pushed one hand through his thick hair and studied Felicity. There was no point in hiding anything from her now; nothing to be gained; but there was no time to be wasted, either. He finished his tea and then dialled his office.

In a moment he was talking to the man who, fairly recently, had become the anchor man at the London headquarters – Chief Inspector Pence. 'You listen,' he told Felicity, and she leaned back, watching him, as he told Pence of the woman's disappearance and to organize a team to go to the nursing home. 'There's a chance that it wasn't Franklin,' he pointed out. 'Whether he took her or not we need a general call out for him.'

'I understand, sir,' Pence said. 'When will you want overseas reports?'

'I'm making up my mind,' Dawlish said.

As they talked and Felicity listened, other things were going on at a different level in Dawlish's mind; for other decisions had to be made and made quickly. And they had to fit in with the curious protocol which had evolved itself within the Metropolitan Police Force, the police forces of the rest of the United Kingdom, and the police forces of the rest of the world. In the beginning a few representatives from some countries had met to discuss not only crimes which crossed borders but crimes which were common to all. Criminals on most levels were using fast means of communication to shift the proceeds of crimes from one nation to another; badly needed criminals were finding it easier to put an ocean between them and the land they were wanted in for major crimes committed. Despite the efforts of Interpol, there had become a sort of clearing house in dozens of countries where criminals could not only dispose of stolen goods quickly but could hold them until they 'cooled' and were safe to sell at large prices, and there were international rings dealing with drugs, currency, jewellery, antiques, paintings, coins – anything of great value.

These 'rings' had grown much as the police organization which had been formed to fight them; slowly but effectively, piece by piece.

The first meeting of the representatives of the international police had been semi-official and advisory; only a dozen countries had been represented. So the International Police Conference was an official organization with a small staff – mostly a secretariat – of its own, its own headquarters in a land-locked African state, and was sponsored by practically every police force in the world, including those politically poles apart.

Moreover each nation now sent its own official delegates to each conference, and contributed to the expenses of the organization.

The conferences could take place in any nation and the police force of the host nation always made the arrangements, while the leading delegate from the host nation was chairman for the actual meeting. In the beginning Scotland Yard had been sceptical but soon it had appointed a permanent delegate with his own offices in London, and the rank of Deputy Assistant Commissioner of the Metropolitan Police Force.

Their choice had been Dawlish.

Dawlish had a long history of experience in espionage and as a kind of unpaid 'private eye'; and this job suited him perfectly, so perfectly that the annual conference of the organization had elected him its permanent chairman and wanted his services full time. No way of arranging that had yet been found, and Dawlish was still a Deputy AC attached to London. But just as his offices were now in a different building, so he had a degree of autonomy as great if not greater than that of the Thames Division.

Co-operation between his own group, known unofficially as the international division, and the Yard and other English police forces was excellent, but it was sometimes slow, and liaison could create exasperating problems.

Dawlish expected none over this, although there had been a time when the Yard had been sceptical. They were the days when the international delegates had been dubbed 'The Crime Haters' by some bright newspapermen, and the name had stuck. Every delegate *was* a crime hater. It was an emotional as well as an intellectual attitude.

All of these things were part of Dawlish; part of his thinking and of his outlook. In a way, too, they were part of Felicity.

At last, Dawlish said into the telephone: 'I would rate the priorities: one, finding any sign of the cloven hoof people; two, finding Lady Franklin; three, finding Sir Justin Franklin.'

'I'll follow that order, sir,' Pence said. 'Gordon Scott was here, he's arranging for the team to go to the clinic. I do think you should come and see the overseas report as quickly as you can, sir – our African headquarters has been on the line about it twice already. I said you would call back.'

'I'll be with you in less than an hour,' Dawlish promised.

'Very good, sir,' Pence replied, and rang off.

Felicity was already getting out of her chair, and

bending across Dawlish for his empty cup. He took unfair advantage for a moment, and then she drew back, laughing, and said: 'Breakfast in twenty minutes – I'd better make it brunch,' and he went into the bathroom, showered first with hot and then with cold water, towelled vigorously, dressed in a well-cut herringbone suit, and then went on to the kitchen. He was sitting at the counter and Felicity was slipping eggs from the frying pan when the front-door bell rang.

Dawlish began to ease off his seat.

'You eat your bacon and eggs while they're hot,' ordered Felicity. She took off a gay, flowered apron and went out. It was years since they had had a sleep-in maid, and their present daily was at home nursing a cold. Dawlish had just helped himself to toast when he heard a sharp explosion, followed by a cry from Felicity.

Off the stool and out of the kitchen in a flash, Dawlish plunged furiously towards the front door.

8   Little Demons

Felicity was standing away from the door with her hands at her face.

There was a smell of burning, and a thin cloud of smoke.

Dawlish reached her in a few long strides, and saw the smoke coming from something smouldering on the floor just outside the door – a tiled floor not in danger of catching fire. The lift doors were closed. He swung round and put an arm about Felicity's shoulder, feeling her shake. But at the same time she managed to say:

'I'm all right, I am really.'

'Let me see your eyes,' Dawlish said, and took her hands away.

Her eyes were swimming with tears but they did not look damaged – certainly there were no cuts or burn marks. He led her back to the kitchen, pressing a bell which rang an alarm in the foyer. It would bring one of his men up very quickly. He took a face cloth and rinsed it in warm water. Felicity took it from him and spread it over her face, pressing gently at her eyes.

'I'm quite all right, you see.'

'Can you tell me what it was?'

'When I opened the door there was – there was a face,' she said. 'A tiny face, it just seemed to be suspended in mid-air. And suddenly it burst into flames. I – I think it was some kind of firework.'

'Firework,' breathed Dawlish only just above his breath.

Felicity took the face cloth away; her eyes were still red-rimmed, and she blinked a lot, but she managed a choking laugh. Dawlish led her to his comfortable chair, then heard men out in the hall.

'Just stay there,' he told her. 'I won't be long.'

He hurried from the kitchen, across the passage to the hall. Two men, both from his Division, were bending over the smouldering mask; its shape was still visible, but now there was very little smoke, although the smell of gunpowder was much stronger.

'From now on I want two men up here and two following my wife wherever she goes,' Dawlish said, abruptly.

'Was she hurt, sir?'

70

'I don't think so. And we need an arson expert to examine this – I'll fix that,' he added. 'You just make sure no one touches it. The ash might be important.' What was the matter with him? Every policeman from the youngest rookie on the Force knew that.

He went back to the kitchen.

Felicity was at the sink, holding an eyebath to one eye, a towel about her shoulders to soak up anything which spilled. She was obviously in complete control of the situation, so he went to the telephone and called the Yard. His chief liaison officer there interrupted before he was halfway through.

'Chief Inspector Fall and an officer from the Fire Department are at the Yard now. Shall I send them over?'

'Please,' Dawlish said. 'How long will they be?'

'I shouldn't think more than twenty minutes,' the other answered.

In fact the two men arrived in eighteen minutes; Fall a very big, rather ungainly man, the officer from the fire service unexpectedly small and dapper. They were already analysing the ash and other salvage from the fire outside the Mandel Clinic, Fall reported, and would analyse this at once. There had been no other reports of fireworks exploding since Guy Fawkes Day.

'And it's the nineteenth now, that's two weeks past,' Fall remarked. For his size he had a very high-pitched voice. 'Shall I send a report to your office or bring it, sir?'

'Send if it's routine, bring if it's unusual,' Dawlish said.

By then Felicity had recovered enough to cook more bacon and eggs and make some toast. Dawlish ate, but had nothing like the appetite he had had before. He had

71

finished except for his second cup of coffee, when he said:

'Hate to say it, darling, but you're going to have shadows wherever you go.'

'Pat – ' She hesitated.

'Yes?'

'That face looked like the face of a little demon.'

'Satyrish,' suggested Dawlish.

'Much more than that; devilish,' she said. 'But – ' She was groping for words and came out with the last one he would have expected: 'Youthful.'

Concealing his anxiety Dawlish said easily: 'Sweetheart, don't go anywhere without making sure your shadows are close behind you. There will be two men in the hall by now and all the time until we clear this damnable business up.'

'Do you think you know any more about it?' Felicity asked, hesitatingly.

'No. Except that I have a feeling that it's coming to a head,' Dawlish said. 'There wouldn't be these attempts to frighten or distract me if it wasn't.' He grinned, and then added in a lighter tone: 'I assure you that in that description no humour is intended! I'll let you know what time I'll be home for dinner.'

He went out of the flat.

Fall and the fire service man had gone; two of his own staff were now on duty, and he gave them simple instructions to check the credentials of anyone who wanted to visit the apartment. Downstairs he found Gordon Scott, showing no sign that he had been up half the night.

'Good morning, sir.'

'Hallo, Gordon. What's brought you?'

'I thought I'd come and try to find out who played

72

that little trick on Mrs Dawlish,' Scott answered, 'but it's very difficult here, as you know.' By day the building was full of office workers and while there was only one lift up to the penthouse there was a fire-escape as well as two air-conditioning shafts and service ladders; anyone could have got up to the penthouse and the 'little devil' was small enough to hide beneath a jacket or in the waistband of a pair of trousers. 'I'm asking all the people in authority if a stranger was noticed.'

'Sounds to me like the old story of the needle and the haystack,' Dawlish said. 'But it's worth finishing.'

Scott said: 'Have you *any* idea what it's about, sir?'

'No,' answered Dawlish, and then added what he had already told Felicity. 'But I have a feeling that it's working up to something.'

'So do at least twenty police forces overseas,' said Gordon Scott, obviously having not the slightest idea of the impact the remark had on Dawlish. 'That's what Pence is so anxious to see you about.'

Chief Inspector Pence was a solid block of a man, his dark hair rapidly turning iron-grey. He had rather heavy, solid-looking features and the mien of a man with little imagination. He had left the Yard several years before and become a security officer at a large aircraft manufacturing and research plant in the English midlands. Because of some strange, and to him inexplicable, events at the plant, he had once come to see Dawlish; and by so doing, staved off a disaster.

Pence had a card-index mind, a well-nigh perfect filing system, and a methodical approach to all problems. It had happened that at the time Dawlish's office chief had retired, Pence had filled the gap, reinstated to the Metropolitan Police as a chief inspector attached to Dawlish. He was in his element. For the African and South American headquarters of the Crime Haters had been beginning, and he had been able to establish a liaison and a system of communications which would have been impossible without him. The South American HQ was run largely by a woman of quite remarkable organizational brilliance. These two had never seen each other but they were in almost daily touch by telephone.

When Dawlish reached his office a little after two o'clock, Pence was in it, sitting at the communications control board in a big room at the top of the Old Scotland Yard building. One side of this room was a huge relief map of the world, on a mercator projection; every mountain and hill, every stream, river and ocean, everything was there – and so were the means of communication: air routes, shipping routes, rail routes. On another wall at right angles to this was another map of the world in four sections, also on a mercator projection. This was a political map, showing all the states, large and small, the cities, towns and villages. And each town or city would light up green if Dawlish or whoever was at the controls wanted to talk to the resident; red, if the resident agent was calling Dawlish.

This system, begun by Dawlish many years ago, had been enlarged and improved by Pence.

He stood up as Dawlish entered the office, poker-faced but affable.

'Good morning, sir. Very glad to see you.'

'I'm sorry I'm late,' said Dawlish. 'What's new?'

Pence said stolidly: 'The usual crimes that you'd expect. And a very much quicker tempo of this devil thing.' When he said 'this devil thing' Pence meant it literally. It was what he had called the affair since it had started. The beginning had been a report of the torture of a young girl from Jaipur, India. There had been a lot of talk of devil worshippers which had strengthened when victims had been found in Haiti, Jamaica, Nairobi and the Sudan.

There had been the sign of the cloven hoof. The physical torture.

There was the fact that every victim suffered some brain damage and many would never recover: would be idiots for the rest of their lives.

Phlegmatic Pence took the view that there was plenty of evidence that the devil worked through human beings, so why not look for those human beings. Within a few days of the first suggestion that there might be a connection between the crimes, descriptions of them had been circulated to every police force in the world with the inevitable request for information about those crimes which might appear to be similar.

At first, reports had merely trickled in; but after a few weeks there had been a steady stream. The common factors had been quickly evident – not only the three which he had already thought about but two others.

Every victim had been a woman.

Every woman had been taken away from her husband or her family.

There was the final factor, as positive now as it had been from the beginning, and yet, contrarily negative.

Not a single motive had been discovered.

The women had been of all races, all religions, all colours; they had come from all stratas of society, high and low. Some had been academically brilliant and some had had an IQ no higher than a schoolgirl of average attainments.

None had been robbed.

Nothing had been stolen from the homes of the victims who had been so grievously maltreated.

There appeared to be no sense in the crimes.

Even now, thinking harder about 'this devil thing' than he had ever done before, Dawlish could see no possible objective. The fact that constant efforts had been made to show the crimes as the work of the devil made no more sense than the rest. These crimes were committed by human agency; Dawlish did not believe in devils any more than Chief Inspector Pence, who was saying:

'We've had fresh reports of these devil things from New York, Johannesburg, Moscow, Buenos Aires, New Delhi and Paris, as well as the two in London last night,' he said, 'and they got up to the same kind of trick in all of these places. Fireworks which burned in the shape of a devil's face, fire and brimstone stuff, and attempts to frighten off the police. Mr Patton in New York thinks they're coming to some kind of climax, and Comrade Poltovitch in Moscow said the same thing.' Pence used 'Comrade' as he would Mr or Herr, or Mynheer: as a courtesy form of address.

'What does Chief Inspector Pence think?' asked Dawlish.

'No thoughts at all,' replied the thickset man, 'except a strong desire to get my hands on them.'

'Have you asked for an analysis of the ash and any wreckage to be relayed here?' asked Dawlish.

'No, I didn't think of it, but it's an idea worth going into,' answered Pence. 'Find out if all these fireworks were manufactured in the same place – that what you mean?'

'Yes.'

76

'I'll fix it,' Pence promised. 'Ought to be done even if it doesn't lead anywhere. Anything else, sir?'

'What do we know about the woman at Epping?'

'A Mrs Gimble, retired housekeeper, ordinary sort of person, nothing special about her as far as we can find out, not a member of any particular club or institution. Just another dead end, so far. There must *be* a connection, sir.'

'Yes,' Dawlish said. 'Where are the cards?'

'On my desk. Like them in?'

'Please,' Dawlish answered.

The 'cards' were simple record cards or dossiers of all the women involved, and every conceivable detail, including likes and dislikes, friends, habits, income, relaxation, health, everything was there. There appeared, however, to be no common denominator.

'But there *must* be,' Dawlish said aloud, and he picked up the newly made-out card for Mrs Rachel Gimble, and read it aloud. A great deal had already been found out about her but there were more gaps on this dossier than on any of the others.

Age: Fifty-four.

Health: Excellent.

Family: Widowed, only son died in car accident in 1961.

Means: Adequate. Works as a daily housekeeper for a solicitor and his family but does not need the money in order to live.

Friends: Mostly church associates and acquaintances.

Recreations: Theatre, cinema, church socials, lectures.

Hobbies: None.

77

Recent Accidents: None.
Scars: None.

There were details of her bank and savings account, of her modest weekly expenditure. There were some reports pending, such as from her dentist and on her condition after she had been found the previous night. One remark in the hand of Dr Mandel's associate said:

Condition poor. Chances of full recovery: small – would be none at all but for her excellent physical condition.

Dawlish felt as if a needle had been stabbed into his mind as he read that last sentence, and then, almost fearfully, turned to other cards and looked for the report on: *Health*. All of the victims had been in excellent physical and mental health. None had scars, so none had ever been operated on. All had excellent, natural teeth, a few with fillings, a few with extractions, but that was all.

The devils!

They were attacking only the healthy!

9   *Good Health!*

Dawlish pushed the report on Mrs Gimble away, and stared at two words he had written on a blank sheet of paper. *Good Health*. After the first flash of excitement he felt a swift deflation. A great many people had good health, it was not really so remarkable. He was snatching at straws, no thing for a policeman to do. He pressed a button which opened a line between him and Pence, in the next room, and Pence answered at once.

'Get me the woman from South America, will you?' Dawlish asked. She had a name which he frequently forgot, though she herself was warmly lodged in his memory. He had found her at the police headquarters of an obscure state in South America, and discovered hers to be the best organizational mind and the best memory of anyone he knew. And now, though living thousands of miles away, on the other side of the equator, she answered in the brightest of voices and in her attractive accent and very personal use of words.

'At last we speak again, Deputy Assistant Commissioner,' she said, and her voice made the receiver sing. 'I am so glad you are well. Now! Please to listen. From more and more places in the world there come the reports. These devil people, they begin to attempt to frighten me. How fools can one be!'

'How many reports are in?' asked Dawlish.

'I can tell you, precisely; thirty-two,' she declared earnestly. 'Also the request made by Signor Pence is now beginning to receive answers, laboratory checks already have been made on some of the ash and some of the material, a plastic, not wholly burnt to destruction. You understand?'

'Perfectly.'

'As gallant as ever, Deputy AC! So – all of the reports which come in are the same.' Her voice rose and fell; a stranger might have thought this was due to excitement, but it was her natural way of speaking. 'A plastic and the explosive used and the burn powder, it would appear we have some good fortune.' Dawlish's heart began to thump. 'All are made in the British colony of Hong Kong, that is now established beyond reasonable doubt.'

'Do we know by whom?' Dawlish demanded.

'As yet, no. There is a supplier of the basic materials and in Hong Kong, as you will be aware, there are hundreds – indeed, thousands – of small merchants and manufacturers. The fact of the origin has been established. So far that is all.'

Dawlish said: 'It's a giant step forward.'

'I will with each new one post you,' she promised.

'Thank you,' Dawlish said mechanically. 'But don't go. And don't laugh.'

'Who am I to laugh in the face of tragedy?' she protested, hotly.

'I think I have found a common factor – that is, a factor common to all the victims.'

'You have?'

'Each one has been in good health: perfect health,' said Dawlish.

He did not know this woman well enough to be quite sure of her reactions and he would not have been surprised had she pooh-poohed his suggestion for its simplicity and obviousness. She did not, in the beginning at least. He heard her heavy breathing as she thought his suggestion over, a miracle over all those thousands of miles which he took absolutely for granted.

Slowly, she said: '*Santa Mari!* Good health!'

'Everyone, without fail. It looks to me as if they select the victims with great care,' Dawlish said.

'And study them perhaps for a long time. Mr Deputy Assistant Commissioner, there is another common fact.

She paused, drawing in her breath, and Dawlish had never gripped the telephone more tightly, nor waited with more intensity. 'All of the victims are *good* people. I do not mean they are all religious or obey the conventions. I mean they are good and kind people,' she told him. 'There is in each report what you call an addendum and this describes all the victims, and this goodness is part of each one. Good health – goodness.'

Dawlish said slowly: 'Have you been converted to a belief that this is the work of the devil?'

'What nonsense to ask!' came the brisk reply. 'I do not know who puts good in some men and evil in others, but I do know that you and I, we are dealing with *men*. You will go to Hong Kong?'

'I may.' Dawlish did not commit himself. 'With luck we'll find the manufacturers and not need to go. If all the things being used are made there and are attributed to them, then they are probably being distributed by air. So we need to have passengers' baggage searched and we need to have all freight examined.' He closed his eyes as he said these things. 'And we can't wait for long.' After another pause he asked: 'How many more new victims are there?'

'Reported today, eleven.'

Dawlish gritted his teeth.

Eleven women, good women in good health – destroyed. Tortured almost beyond human understanding and *destroyed*. How many more would go today? Was he right and were the others right in believing this was building up to a climax?

Another thought flashed, not new, one which had at times driven him to a frenzy because he could not answer it, and which came now with an even greater, more sickening force. How could those who were to

81

become victims today be saved? So far not a single one had been; nor had a single perpetrator been caught.

'I have been thinking – ' he said.

'Yes, Mr Deputy Assistant Commissioner?'

'We still need some common factor which distinguishes the victims in advance.'

'We still look.'

'But have we looked close enough? What they wear, where they have been in the past few years or even weeks, where – ' He broke off, for he had said these things so often that there was no sense in repeating them. Yet the darkness, the obscurity of the affair, goaded him beyond endurance. Yesterday eleven women had been walking about freely, living their normal daily lives, happy as far as anyone knew, unaware of the disaster which was to strike.

At this moment there might be a dozen more who were living their last normal day on earth, who that day or that night would be so branded after such torture that their minds would virtually die.

Good people.

Healthy people.

Happy people.

Oh, God in heaven, *why*?

And *who*? Who would be next? If only he had the slightest idea, if only there was something he and the thousands working with him could do to warn, to save, them.

Lisa Day was just twenty-four.

She was an attractive woman with honey-coloured hair and brown, laughter-wrinkled eyes: and she laughed a great deal, for she was a happy person.

She would have been astonished had she been told

82

that she was also good, but a dozen of her closer associates at the City of London office where she worked would undoubtedly have described her as 'good' had they been asked. Happy, generous, likable, *good*; the one person to whom everyone could turn for help, be it for a little money to tide one over a bad patch, a sympathetic ear, or a warm understanding. There was nothing spectacular about her, not even about her looks: she just had a warming effect on people – men and women alike.

About the time that Dawlish was on the telephone talking to the woman from South America, she was in her office in one of the smaller new buildings in the City, not far from the Bank. She was secretary to three of the salesmen in the company, General Supplies Limited, which dealt in a great variety of goods, importing and exporting them throughout the world. She handled the correspondence for the three salesmen when they were away – for each one spent much time abroad. In this, the management had complete confidence in her and was more likely to ask for information or advice than to question what she was doing.

A man walked past her desk and then turned back and spoke to her.

'Are you busy tonight, Lisa?'

'Very busy,' she declared.

'Too busy to come out to dinner with me?' he asked. He was in his fifties, grey-haired, handsome, but curiously weak-looking.

'I'm sorry, Paul,' she said, 'but I've a date for dinner.'

'Lucky young pup,' the man Paul said. 'Do I know him?'

'Ah,' said Lisa gaily, 'that would be telling!'

Both of them laughed, and the man went on.

Lisa bent over her typewriter with renewed energy.

She was in the middle of a letter which was in the form of a report to Russell Cartwright, one of the three men whose work she shared. He was both buyer and seller in the Far East for every conceivable kind of consumer goods, from wooden toys to transistor radios, from metal and plastic pots and pans to cheap cutlery, from cameras and flashlight bulbs to fireworks.

She was telling him what orders had come in during the past week, and what inquiries for various goods. It was not a particularly long letter, and both matter-of-fact and friendly. The last paragraph was not about business at all. It said:

I talked to Rosemary (Russell Cartwright's wife) this morning and she seemed so busy – but she really does miss you terribly. . . . And believe it or not, I have a new admirer. What an old-fashioned word! He is – wait for it – a policeman! Well, a detective, really. So I shall have to watch my p's and q's.

Hope you're well. Be *very* good!

Lisa

She read the letter through and then put it back in the machine and added a postscript:

The consignment of masks and fireworks arrived and were sent on by special delivery, but I don't think you will be able to handle this line much longer. There were so many deaths and injuries this Guy Fawkes Day that there is a great outcry to ban not only imports but manufacture, except under the strictest control.

L.

84

Satisfied, she addressed the envelope, dropped it into her box-file of other letters, and began to deal with orders. These were processed here at the head office and sent through to a variety of warehouses outside London, where costs were generally lower.

She kept her mind on the job, banishing all thoughts of Bob. That was for this evening; he would meet her at six o'clock at the Waldorf Hotel, which she knew as being neither too expensive nor too popular. There was a pleasant lounge with music, where they would have drinks. The rest of the evening would look after itself.

It was nearly five o'clock. She would be free to leave the office in half an hour. She was looking forward to it.

Did this mean that Bob meant much more than anyone else had?

In turn, Detective Sergeant Robert Harrison was *not* keeping his mind on his job.

He thought a great deal about Lisa, and although he told himself he was a fool, even thinking of her could make his heart miss a beat. It was not as if he knew nothing of women or of sex – sex, as the world said today, for fun. He was thirty-one, with above average intelligence, a good body which he kept in good condition. Not too much drink, no smoking except an occasional evening cigar, temperate in everything except his hatred of crime.

That was why he had always wanted to be transferred to the international division, under Dawlish. How one got there he had no idea, for twice he had made tentative inquiries and each time he had been told evasively:

'The great Dawlish picks his own men.'

'But how?' Bob Harrison had demanded.

'You'd better ask Dawlish,' his then sergeant had replied, drily.

He had written to Dawlish twice and received polite acknowledgements: his application would be filed.

He little guessed how soon that chance would come. Sitting in the office which he shared with five other sergeants in Holborn, brooding equally over Lisa Day and the Crime Haters, he was in a position to receive an urgent telex message. It was headed *Highly Confidential* and read:

> Information is urgently needed about importers of fireworks, plastic toys and masks and other small plastic items which are imported from Hong Kong. An explosion occurred outside the Mandel Clinic, Weybridge Street, W.1. in the early hours of the morning caused by such a mask and a smaller explosion and fire was caused at the house of Deputy Assistant Commissioner Dawlish at noon today.
>
> Comprehensive lists of importers are being prepared but officers who may have information which would enable checks to be made quickly should report at once to Chief Inspector Pence, DAC's office.

Bob Harrison read this again, and breathed: 'That's the way into the Crime Haters!' A moment later he thought: 'Lisa's firm deals with Hong Kong and she said something about fireworks the other day. My God! This may be what I've been waiting for!'

10   Clue?

Harrison could do two things.

He could call Chief Inspector Pence and tell him what he knew so far, which wasn't very much really, or he could ask Lisa a lot of questions tonight and try to find out all he could about the 'fireworks' her boss handled. What was the man's name? Had she ever mentioned it? Had she mentioned *any* names?

Take it easy, Harrison cautioned himself.

It was then half past four and he had an hour and a quarter before he needed to leave for the Waldorf. He could call and ask Lisa if she could get away early, but she would want to know why, and he could hardly tell her the truth over the telephone. Half an hour wouldn't make much difference, either.

How would Lisa respond to being questioned? She had mentioned casually the importing of fireworks from Hong Kong after the tragic experiences of Guy Fawkes night, adding that, as he probably knew, the Chinese were experts in every form of explosive toy.

Keep your mind on your job!

He gave an unnecessary cough, part-excitement, part-admonitory. But supposing, by ingratiating himself into the good books of the Crime Haters, he put himself into Lisa's bad books? Of course, if he could tell her what it was about – ah! *There* was a good reason for checking with the man Pence first, for the message was, after all, marked *Highly Confidential*. He glanced across at his fellow sergeant who was engrossed in making out a report, lifted his own receiver and gave the number of Dawlish's office.

87

'I'll give you a line,' his operator said.

So he dialled.

The dialling sound went on for a long time, and he was beginning to think he had dialled the wrong number when there was a break in the ringing and a man said in a deep voice:

'Dawlish.'

Dawlish stabbed through Harrison's mind. This was the great Dawlish himself, who would have dreamt that he would answer the telephone? *Dawlish.* He gulped – and the man at the other end of the line said:

'This is Deputy Assistant Commissioner Dawlish – can you hear me?'

Harrison gulped again, and managed to say: 'I – I wanted Chief Inspector Pence.'

'He's engaged. Can I give him a message?'

'Er – ' began Harrison, and hissed to himself: 'Get a grip on yourself.' He drew a deep breath and then spoke more clearly: 'It's about a teletype message which has just come round, sir – I'm at the Holborn Station.'

'The Hong Kong memo?' asked Dawlish, and there was no doubt at all about the sharpening of his tone.

'Yes, sir.'

'Go on,' Dawlish ordered, and his manner sounded ominous.

'I – er – I'm Detective Sergeant Harrison, CID, sir. This may be absolutely nothing at all, but' – *get a grip on yourself* – 'it so happens that a friend of mine – girl-friend – works for a company which does a lot of business with Hong Kong and her actual boss is there at the moment. It came out in conversation, sir, that he sent back a special box of masks and fireworks recently. She mentioned it because of the Guy Fawkes night trouble. I'm due to see her again tonight and I could find out more but – well, she may not like being pumped, sir. Questioned. I wondered if I could tell her why I needed to know. I'm sure she would co-operate fully once she knew.'

'Yes,' Dawlish said without hesitation. 'Show her the telex message if it will help, and report here, please, the moment you've formed an opinion one way or the other.'

'Oh, I will!' promised Harrison, fervently. 'Thank you very much, sir.'

'Goodbye,' Dawlish said, and rang off.

Harrison replaced the receiver slowly.

He had kept his voice low and had no idea whether the other sergeant knew whom he had been talking to. He could hardly believe it. And for Dawlish to take him seriously! It was like a miracle.

He sat looking down at the message; a lean, healthy-looking, fresh-faced man with nearly red hair and narrow features. When he stood up his leanness made him look even taller than his six feet two inches. He folded the message, a copy of which had been put on each desk, and went out. It was now getting on for five o'clock, and only an hour before his rendezvous.

He must go and meet Lisa.

She preferred him not to, and he respected that decision, but, surely, this time it was different. She would leave the office sharp at half past five, so he need not start immediately. She would walk to the Waldorf, that was an easy half-hour's walk, and he could follow and catch up with her at the Bank, say. Or at St Paul's, that would be better, she couldn't possibly mind that. He was already officially off duty, and so he had a cup of tea in the canteen, and then set out to walk to the

89

City. There were a dozen short cuts which he knew well, and he walked between old buildings and new, across main roads and along narrow alleys until, at twenty-five past five, he reached Billington Street opposite the entrance to Billington House. General Supplies Limited were on the top three floors of this building, and, except for the fire exit at the back, there was only one entrance. Harrison stepped into the porch of an old building, and waited.

Several other people, he noticed, were also waiting, standing about on both sides of the street. Traffic passed, heading east, in a constant stream. The narrow pavements, already crowded with homegoers, became more and more crowded as the offices which closed at half past five began to empty.

Several Chinese were among the passers-by; and at least one of them was waiting on the far side of the street.

Harrison did not give these men a thought, could think only of Lisa. When she was five minutes late he began to worry in case she had left a few minutes early and he had lost her, but suddenly his heart expanded and a fatuous grin spread over his face.

There she was!

Dressed in a grey tweed suit, skirt swinging as she walked, a scarf loose about her neck and shoulders, an umbrella in her left hand, handbag in her right. She looked absolutely enchanting, as if this were the beginning of the day rather than the end.

She turned left, towards the Bank.

Afterwards, when full realization dawned, he admitted that it was almost incredible, but it was a fact that at that stage he did not notice that she was being followed by the Chinaman who had been standing near the entrance; nor did he notice with any significance that a man, who might have been any office worker, was more or less keeping pace with him. After a while he became aware of this man, but there were several others walking at about the same pace, and there was nothing particularly surprising about it.

He noticed the taxi.

It was parked some distance along on Lisa's side of the road, where no vehicle was supposed to stand during the rush hour. Lisa, walking forward, was then hidden by it. On that instant, a man on the other side of the street shouted, and, beyond the taxi, fell heavily, knocking into several people before he hit the ground. In no time at all there was a tight-packed crowd, unable to pass in one direction or the other, and because of this Lisa was not visible.

Across the street a voice was raised:

'Is there a doctor here? Is there a doctor?'

Another man said in a carrying voice: 'Some kind of fit.'

The crowd on either side of the taxi grew thicker. A few people stepped into the road so as to pass, car horns honked in loud protest. Two police helmets showed above the crowd, but Bob Harrison stayed where he was.

All he wanted was to see Lisa.

Suddenly the taxi started off, and a policeman held up traffic behind it to allow the vehicle to get into the main stream. Once it had gone, at least a hundred people were jammed in the narrow pavement, held up by the fallen man and the crowd who would not move away. A policeman began to call:

'Pass along, please. Move along.'

Harrison could not see Lisa.

At first this did not really worry him, for there were dozens of women in the crowd, some pushed into doorways, others into shops. She would appear at any moment. The police cordoned off a small section of the road and one constable directed the traffic to the other side. In the distance came the ringing of an ambulance bell.

There was still no sign of Lisa, and now Harrison began to feel worried. He nipped in front of an oncoming bus to the other side of the road, and as he reached the far kerb a man who had been on the ground until that moment, obviously the victim of the fit, leapt to his feet. It was a stupendous piece of acrobatics. On his back one moment he was upright the next, dodging the heads of several people who had been bending over him, pushing them aside, then racing along the road between the kerb and the stream of cars and buses.

No one except Harrison had the slightest chance of catching him.

Harrison turned on the ball of his foot and began to run. As he did so, the truth began to seep into his mind, and it was a frightening truth. That taxi, the man with the fit, everything had been skilfully planned to enable the men to take Lisa away.

She had been hustled into the taxi.

What else could it mean?

He was beginning to gasp for breath, but the other man must be flagging, too, and he believed he could see the taxi which had started all the trouble. He redoubled his efforts, praying for his second wind, when someone at the side shot out a leg and he kicked against it and went sprawling. It was so sudden and unexpected that he had no chance to protect his head

92

as he fell against the kerb. He did not lose consciousness, but a thousand lights appeared behind his eyes, while a splitting pain seemed to divide his skull in two.

Slowly the lights dimmed and the pain eased; less slowly, he began to realize exactly what had to be done. He clutched the arm of a City of London policeman who was helping him up.

'I must talk to the International Brigade at once.'

'To the *what*, sir?'

'I am – ' Harrison took out a card and showed it, fought back a fresh wave of pain in his head, and went on: 'You know. The International Brig – '

'I know, Sergeant,' the City man said. 'Can you walk? I'll get you to a telephone in two jiffs.'

Dawlish was looking through the time-tables of flights to Hong Kong.

He wasn't yet absolutely sure that he should go but he would decide before the next flight. He needed only half an hour to pack, and Felicity would come to the airport with him. He wanted to hear what the man Harrison had to report, acknowledging that it was probably one of a thousand false leads which came in every day. Sooner or later there had to be a winner.

His telephone bell rang.

This time it was from the operator here; earlier, when Harrison had telephoned, Dawlish had just finished a call which he had dialled direct; it was a sheer fluke that he had answered. Well, sheer flukes had convicted a host of criminals.

'Yes,' he said.

'It's a Sergeant Harrison, sir, he says – '

'Put him through!' barked Dawlish. It was too early for Harrison to have any news – damn it, it wasn't yet six o'clock; but why should the man call unless he had something to say? He had obviously been nervous, had probably forgotten something he now regarded as important.

'Mr Dawlish?' Harrison's voice was unmistakable yet there was a different tone in it: Dawlish thought, trouble; and he buzzed for Pence to listen in as he said: 'Yes.'

'I have good reason to believe that Miss Day, Lisa Day, has been kidnapped,' declared Harrison. 'There was a disturbance in Billington Street caused by a man who pretended to have a fit. Miss Day was hidden during the early part of the disturbance by a taxi cab . . .' He told his story with commendable lucidity but at the same time conveyed an impression of very great tension. 'I have the number of the taxi and also a description of the man who faked a fit. I've given the number to the City Police, and they . . .'

Three minutes later, Dawlish said: 'When you've done all you can wherever you are, come here, will you? I'll fix it with your Divisional Superintendent.'

Harrison said: 'Yes, sir.'

He was about to realize the greatest ambition of his life, and he did not get the slightest thrill out of it. All he felt was a terrible fear for Lisa.

11   Kidnap

No police force in the world could work more swiftly or with greater impact once it was roused. Already alerted by what had happened to Lady Franklin, the Assistant Commissioners for Crime and Uniform at Scotland Yard, the City of London Police, and the police in the counties bordering London, needed only a signal to swing into action.

Dawlish's call to the Assistant Commissioner for Crime at Scotland Yard was that signal. Within minutes a description of the taxi, its number, its driver and passenger, was flashed to all of these forces. So was a description of the man who had feigned a fit. Every policeman, from the beat to the senior superintendents, took time to help in the search, and they were aided by the fact that there had been a big traffic hold-up at Aldgate Pump at the time of Lisa Day's disappearance, and four uniformed policemen and two plain-clothes men had noticed the taxi because of the driver.

He was Chinese – or Oriental – for certain; and there were very few such taxi-drivers in London.

The number of the taxi which Harrison reported was XL543Y; a policeman alerted by the general call saw a cab with a Chinese driver at Whitechapel Church at six-twenty with the number AB721X. He would not have noted this but for the call. Search for cab XL543Y was fruitless; no one else saw it. But police in the East End of London saw a cab answering the description – a black Beardmore with a big scratch on one wing – with the number AB721X.

'Not much doubt it switched numbers while moving,' a traffic superintendent told Dawlish.

'Do you know where it is now?'

'Near Camberwell Green, sir.'

'For God's sake don't lose it!'

'No one's going to lose it,' he was assured.

He put down the telephone in his office as there came a tap at the door, and on his 'come in' Pence appeared, slow-moving and deliberate as ever.

'Will you try for that eight o'clock flight now, sir?'

'No,' Dawlish said. 'We might have struck oil.'

'Please God,' said Pence with unexpected fervour. 'Detective Sergeant Harrison is here, sir.'

'Ah,' said Dawlish. 'What's he like?'

'I like the look of him, sir, but – '

'But what?'

'He's upset,' stated Pence without hesitation.

'Can we be surprised?' asked Dawlish.

'Will he be able to give us all he's got, sir?'

'Possibly that, and a bit more if he's in love with the girl. Have you told him what we now know happened in Billington Street?'

'No, sir.'

'I will,' Dawlish said. 'Before you send him in, are there any other reports?'

'Nothing new from overseas,' Pence assured him, 'but several more of the same thing. *Information* tells me they've got that cab pinpointed so well that they're sometimes getting three reports about it in the same minute.'

Dawlish said: 'Excellent. All right, I'll see Harrison.'

He understood what Pence meant when he said he liked the look of the young sergeant; it was a quality hard to define, an impression of reliability and of honesty but much more than that. He could also see telltale signs of tension at the rather full lips, strange in a lean face; and there was no doubt about the anxiety in his eyes.

'Come in, Harrison,' Dawlish said, and as the man moved forward, he went on: 'I'm sorry about your young woman, but it must be a relief to know there isn't a policeman in or near London who isn't keeping an eye open for her.'

'Is there any news, sir?' Harrison asked quietly.

'Some old news, and some up-to-date news of the taxi,' Dawlish said. 'It's a good job you spotted that. We think it changed numbers soon after driving off, and that we know exactly where it is. We can't be sure who is inside it, since there was a time gap between the moment Miss Day was seen getting into the cab, and – '

'She was actually *seen*, sir?' Harrison's voice rose.

'Yes. That is what I mean by the old news. When she was held up by the disturbance created by the thrower of fits, she was apparently pushed towards the taxi and was either made to get in or got in of her own accord. Accounts vary, as most of the people were interested in the man they thought was in a fit. Most of them, I fear, were only interested in how long it would delay them.' Dawlish paused, but Harrison showed no reaction, so Dawlish went on: 'There was a man in the taxi – a white man, not a Chinese like the driver and the thrower of fits. And there was another man on the pavement who took Lisa Day's elbow and apparently helped – or forced – her into the taxi. Two of the witnesses say she looked scared, each thought that the sight of the man on the pavement was enough to cause that. It wasn't until we began to question them that the picture as I'm giving it to you took shape.'

Harrison said huskily: 'I understand that, sir.'

'Have you any idea at all what it's all about?' asked Dawlish. 'Had she confided in you at all – more than you've already told me, I mean?'

97

'No, sir. She never talks about her work except in the most general terms – she is secretary . . .' He explained what little he knew and added: 'I don't even know the names of any of the men she works for. The business of a special consignment of fireworks coming by air came out almost accidentally, sir. Just because we were talking about the tragedies on Guy Fawkes night.'

A buzzer sounded on Dawlish's desk.

There was an urgency in the sound, and just how urgent only Dawlish knew, for Pence would not have interrupted him during this interview unless he felt it was a matter of extreme importance. So he murmured: 'Sorry about this. . . . Hallo, Chief Inspector.'

'That cab's gone to earth,' Pence announced in the clearest of voices. 'It's in the garage of a house between Camberwell and Peckham. Big house in its own grounds. Two men and a woman were last seen in the cab as it turned into the drive, but there was no time for identification. The Yard's really gone to town, sir. There are three cordons round the place – one in nearby streets, one at all main roads, one at all main road junctions. The Assistant Commissioner says will you take over, sir – on the spot.'

Dawlish said: 'Have a car waiting.' He put down the receiver and said in a surprisingly quiet voice to Harrison: 'We think we've found her but there's no certainty. You can come if you carry out every order that I give you implicitly.'

Harrison said stiffly: 'All I want is to get her safe. I can't help thinking that it was I who got her into this.'

It did not occur to Lisa Day that what happened to

98

her was even remotely to do with Bob Harrison.

At first, the hold-up had been merely exasperating: a delay on an evening when she did not want to lose a moment. Then she had seen the man on the ground, writhing, hands and teeth clenched, foam at his mouth, and she had thought: Epileptic, and wondered what she could do to help. Someone ought to put something into his hands to prevent him from digging his nails into the palms, for instance, and a wedge between his teeth.

She tried to get nearer, but the crush of people was so great that she could not make any headway. It was almost as if one man was deliberately pushing her towards the kerb, but she could not be sure. Men and women were grumbling, fearful of missing trains and buses, and those coming from behind seemed to have no sense at all, they just pushed into the crowd that was already too thick.

Suddenly a hand closed about her arm.

'What on earth – ' she began angrily, for this was no accident.

'Don't talk, don't shout, get into the taxi,' the man holding her said.

His voice was low-pitched and his mouth so close to her ear that she could feel the hot breath. *Ugh*! She tried to draw her hand away, but as she did so the man tightened his grip and twisted – and pain shot up her forearm to her shoulder.

'You'll really get hurt if you don't do what I tell you.' She no longer had the slightest doubt that he meant what he said.

She kicked him.

He gasped in turn and for a moment his grip slackened, but as she pulled herself free, another man appeared at her other side and gripped her wrist in exactly the same way. He did not speak, but twisted, and the pain made her go limp with the shock. Then she was aware of a hand at each elbow, of men pushing her towards the cab, of pain where they gripped so excruciating that she stepped blindly into the taxi, ready to do anything to stop them from hurting her any more. Next she saw a man inside the cab, hands stretched forward to pull her in as one of the men behind gave her a shove.

She staggered; and the man inside pushed her on to the seat beside him, while one of the others got into the cab and sat on one of the tip-up seats. Almost at once the cab started off. She actually saw a policeman holding up traffic so that it could get away, but she could do nothing; the man who had been in the car held her so tightly that she was unable to struggle; and could only watch, terrified, the hypodermic syringe approaching her arm. She thought hazily of flinging herself at the window, of pulling it down and screaming for help, but she had no strength. She tried to cry out, but knew that she made only whimpering noises. Suddenly, consciousness left her.

The man who had given her the injection said: 'She won't give any more trouble.'

'How long will she be out?'

'Long enough.'

'He'll want to question her.'

'She won't be out too long.' The man was putting his hypodermic syringe away. The lid of the box snapped shut as he turned towards the partition between passengers and driver, and asked sharply: 'Have you changed the number plates?'

'Number plates changed, sir,' the driver answered.

'Are we being followed?'

'No sign we are being followed, sir.'

'What about the man who ran after us?'

'Man who ran after us had unfortunate accident and fell to ground,' the driver answered. 'Man fell over another man's leg.'

The man on the tip-up seat gave an ugly laugh. 'We're in the clear.' He stretched out his legs. They were in Whitechapel by then, and soon driving through the Rotherhithe Tunnel on the circuitous drive to Camberwell. They passed policemen unaware that their progress was being reported, and that they were followed.

The house they reached after fifty minutes' driving was of an unlovely Victorian period, a survival of the days when this area had been residential and many big houses had been built here for the owners and managers of the countless factories in the East End of London. A large garage stood with the doors open.

Lisa Day stirred.

Neither of the men who had travelled with Lisa now touched her. Two men, one an Englishman and one a Chinese, lifted her out of the cab and into the house. Soon, they turned into a small room on the second floor, and laid her on a narrow bed.

The room seemed full of electrical machines and wires, and in one glass-fronted cabinet there were hypodermic syringes, and a pile of ampoules. For a few moments the girl was left alone. She turned her head from side to side but did not regain consciousness. A middle-aged woman and an elderly man came in, both white, both wearing surgical smocks. They began to undress Lisa, methodically and slowly. She was now dressed in the briefest of underclothes.

Standing on either side of the bed, the man and woman passed a canvas belt beneath the bed and over her body; it was no more than two inches wide but it held her securely.

She began to stir, and her eyes opened, closed, and opened again. Neither of the others took any notice, but went out of the room and left her alone, closing the door. The only light came from a small fluorescent strip above the door and it gave an eerie, greenish glow.

She lay very still for a while as full consciousness returned. She could see the room and the electric machines; she could even see the cabinet with the hypodermic needles. She tried to sit up, but the belt was too tight and all she could do was raise her head and see her legs, the belt, her body. She dropped back on the pillow, terrified. She could remember everything so vividly: the man who had been taken ill, the pain of the man's grip, the sharp stab of the injection –

How long had she been unconscious?

Why had they brought her here?

What were they going to do with her?

As the questions came into her mind, she felt an agonising stab of pain, at her shoulders, at her thighs, up and down her legs, and she opened her mouth and screamed. The screaming seemed to echo back at her from the bare walls, as if sneering at her.

The pain stopped, but it was different now, she was quivering and on edge because she knew there might be more pain, that she was utterly helpless. It was as if she had been brought here for an experiment. She couldn't bear –

The pain struck like red-hot wires drawn through her body.

She screamed again.

Then the door opened and two men came in. She did not know whether these were the pair who had been in the taxi with her, because they wore smocks, and surgical masks. She could only just see their eyes. Even the voice of the man who spoke was distorted by the mask – unless he deliberately distorted it so that she would not be able to recognize it again.

'Now, we have some questions to ask you,' he said, 'and we want the answers quickly. If we have to wait more than nine seconds for a reply you will get another dose of this.'

She felt a sharp stab of pain – bad but not unbearable, not enough to make her scream. She looked towards him, sweat pouring down her face, and she begged as Ursula Franklin had begged:

'Don't hurt me. If I can tell you anything I will. I swear I will!'

12   Action

The car in which Dawlish and Harrison had come was parked three streets away from the house where Lisa had been taken; a long narrow street in which most of the old houses had been turned into flatlets, where children played noisily, and where only a few front gardens still boasted trees and shrubs. Police in plain clothes were at various vantage points, some on the roofs of the taller buildings, some blocking off every possible way of escape for the people at the house, which was known as The Elms, Ford Street.

All of these things had been flashed by Dawlish on the way, and Harrison knew as much about the situation as Dawlish himself. The younger man was obviously tense but showed no signs of allowing emotion to take control of him.

A superintendent, big, burly-looking, with keen, intelligent eyes and a deep, pleasing voice, now stood by the side of the car talking to Dawlish, who had introduced Harrison without much explanation.

'As I see the situation, sir, if we raid the house they might harm the young woman,' said the superintendent. 'They've been pretty ruthless so far, it seems.'

Dawlish nodded.

'Sooner or later we ought to raid,' went on the superintendent, 'but should we try reasoning with them first?'

'Give her, and yourselves, up and all will be forgiven,' Dawlish said with forced lightness.

'They'd get more consideration that way, anyhow,' the superintendent declared, obviously nettled.

Dawlish's smile did nothing to change the bleakness of his eyes. 'I know enough about these people to be pretty sure they won't listen to reason,' he said. 'We need someone in the house to find where Miss Day is, and when we've done that we must raid.'

'I'd like to volunteer, sir.' Harrison spoke very quietly. 'It won't surprise them to see me – I did start by giving chase, after all. And I've strong personal reasons, as you know.'

'There will be plenty of opportunities for you to pull off long shots, Sergeant,' Dawlish said gently, 'but this isn't one of them. I shall go.'

'But, sir!' protested the superintendent.

'Very much my job,' Dawlish said, in a tone which brooked no argument. 'Two things. I need a taxi, quickly, driven by one of our men – it can wait for me at the house and yes, no reason why one of our chaps shouldn't hide in the cab, in case I need sudden help on my way out. And there's an outside chance that the house is full of fireworks and could go up in flames, so we ought to make sure that two or three firefighting units are at hand. Can you fix these?'

The superintendent said, reluctantly: 'Well, if you insist.' He gave an order to a detective sergeant who was standing by and who said:

'No problem with the taxi, sir. We've two along here.'

'May I drive the taxi?' asked Harrison. His voice quivered as he spoke, and his lean face had a beseeching expression.

'They might recognize you,' said Dawlish. 'But you can be the man who hides inside.'

'You might get away with passenger and driver,' said the superintendent, 'but if there's someone on the floor and one of the men from the house takes a peak, then the game will be up.'

'I just can't stand by doing nothing!' Harrison burst out.

The expression on the burly superintendent's face seemed to say: 'You would if you were in my division.' Aloud he said: 'I could find plenty of volunteers, sir.'

'You're very good,' Dawlish said. 'But I'd be happier doing it my way.'

Within two minutes an older taxi than the one in which Lisa had been kidnapped turned out of a side street, and drew up alongside. The driver got down, opened the back door, and leaned inside; he pulled at the rear seat and it came up like a lid. 'Room for a little 'un in there, sir,' he said. 'Plenty of air holes.' He was a small man for a policeman and there was a twinkle in his eyes.

'In you get,' Dawlish said to Harrison.

Soon he was turning into Ford Street, hearing the shouts of children playing in the light of the lamps. They turned into The Elms, and the dimmed headlights of the taxi shone on a dark front door which needed painting, and two scabrous porch pillars.

There was absolutely no way of telling what would happen next.

Lisa Day lay there, helpless.

Her mouth was parched, sometimes she could hardly get words out.

Now and again when she had taken a long time to answer a question a stab of pain had shot through her body, but she had had sufficient respite to know that this was caused by electric currents touching sensitive nerve spots, strong enough at times to make her want to arch her body; but for the restraint of the straps she would have.

The two men were still there, and she had no idea who they were.

She had answered every question – hating herself.

For the questions had mostly been about Bob.

How long had she known him. . . . Were they lovers? *No.* Were they going to be? *She didn't know.* How much had she told him about business? *Nothing.* Absolutely nothing? *Yes, she –*

Pain had exploded inside her, and after a few moments the same man had put the question again:

106

How much have you told him about business? . . . *Practically nothing.* . . . How much? had come with another stab of pain. . . . *I mentioned the special consignment from Hong Kong* . . . Did you say who had consigned it? . . . *No.* . . . What else had she told him about business? . . . *Nothing.* . . . If she lied she would wish she had never been born, remember that. . . . How many questions had he asked her about General Supplies Limited? . . . *Nothing!* . . . Be careful and don't forget anything else: how much had she told him about 'her' three salesmen? . . . *Nothing.* . . . How much about senior management? . . . *Nothing. I swear, nothing.* . . . You're a spy for the police, aren't you? . . . *No. No. Don't hurt me, don't* . . .

It was like being flung into a fire, and this time the recovery took much longer. And soon she was able to understand the man again, and he began to ask the same questions. Panic flooded through her because she knew that if an answer varied from any she had ever given then that awful burning would come again.

Then the man who had asked the questions said: 'She's telling the truth, I'm sure about that.'

Thank God, thank God, they were going to stop this awful torture.

The other asked: 'What shall we do with her?'

The first man laughed. 'Give her the treatment, we can't risk her talking.' He stood at the side of the bed and the other man stood at the foot until he turned slowly and opened the glass case where she had seen the hypodermic needles.

Dawlish's taxi drew up outside the front door of The Elms, and he got out and went straight to the porch and rang the bell. He was aware of shadowy figures

107

in the grounds, saw one man actually go close to the taxi and peer inside, then move away.

Dawlish rang again, and the door opened; a small man, Chinese, perhaps, certainly Oriental, stood there.

'Good evening.'

'Good evening,' Dawlish said, and stepped inside. There was so little time.

If there was a way of finding the girl it was by the roughest of tactics, tactics he was more expert in than any man he knew. The little man was now protesting: 'You must not do that, you are not allowed to.' Dawlish took the man's arm, twisted him round and thrust the arm upwards in a hammerlock. 'Take me to the woman.'

The man gasped: 'No woman here, sir. No – '

Dawlish thrust his arm up even further, and he gasped as if in anguish. A man appeared at one of the doors leading into the hall. Dawlish took a gun from his pocket and aimed. There was a soft *zutt* of sound and the 'bullet' struck the door frame and burst, giving off a cloud of tear gas vapour. As he moved forward up the stairs yet another man appeared at their head; this time a tear-gas pellet struck him before he could move away and he gasped and backed, hands at his face.

'*Where is she?*' demanded Dawlish. '*Tell me. Where is she?*' He released the man he had frog-marched only to seize him again and hoist him high above his head; only a man of Dawlish's great strength could have done this even with a small man. 'Where is she? Tell me or I'll throw you down the stairs.' He actually moved the victim backwards as if in preparation and the man gasped:

'No, no! I tell, I tell!'

He pointed up to a second landing.

As they reached it, a scream came harsh and hideous across the quiet; and Dawlish no longer doubted that the other was telling the truth. He gave the man a chopping blow on the back of the neck; he collapsed, without a sound.

The scream came again.

Dawlish dared not run, too much noise would warn whoever was in the room with her. He crept close to the walls, nearing a brighter light beneath the door from which the screaming had come. Now he could hear the words.

'No, no, *no!*'

A man said roughly: 'Hold her still, or – '

Dawlish turned the handle and opened the door.

The bed was facing him, and he saw the near naked girl on it, saw the terror in her eyes, the sweat which glistened on her body and matted her hair, and for a split second thought: Thank heavens Harrison didn't come. Neither of the men had seen him. One had a hypodermic needle poised over her, the other was holding her shoulders and pressing them down.

He said: 'Enough, I think.'

As both men swung round, he launched himself at the one with the syringe and struck the forearm savagely; the syringe fell. Dawlish hit him with all the strength he could find, strength the greater because of the surging hatred he felt for them both.

The other man rushed at him.

Dawlish simply kicked him in the groin; heard the impact and the harsh intake of breath, saw him double up and then sway against the wall. The other man lay still. Dawlish stretched across and turned the key in the lock of the door, then bent over the girl.

109

'It's all right,' he said, gently. 'No one's going to hurt you any more. It's all right.'

He found the buckle of the strap and unfastened it and then put his arms beneath her, feeling the mattress wet with sweat. He lifted her gently, and supported her to a hand basin in a corner near the drug cupboard; there was a sponge, towels, soap. He ran warm water on to the sponge, talking soothingly all the time as he wiped her forehead, face and neck, her shoulders and her breasts; cooling her body. He heard shouting outside on the landing but ignored it, he rinsed the sponge out and repeated what he had already done, talking all the time.

'No one is going to hurt you any more. . . . Bob will soon be here. . . . Everything is all right now.' She looked at him but did not try to speak. He filled a glass with water and held it to her mouth, supporting her head.

Footsteps thundered on the stairs, a fist thumped on this door.

'Open up or I'll break the door down!' Harrison roared.

Dawlish called: 'All right, Sergeant. I'll come and unlock it.' He looked down at Lisa Day, smiled, and draped the largest towel round her shoulders. Then he crossed to the door and unlocked it. Detective Sergeant Robert Harrison stood there.

'Now take it easy,' Dawlish cautioned. 'Just sponge her face and forehead until a doctor comes. But she's all right,' he added with assurance. 'She had a rough time but she's all right.'

Then Harrison came in – and saw not only Lisa but the two men on the floor.

Three plain-clothes policemen were on this landing,

110

forcing open another door. More police were on the one below. Dawlish felt as if his knees would bend and he would fall. A man put out a hand to steady him but he did not notice. He gripped the handrail at the side of the stairs and went down very slowly, step by step. Not only the tremendous physical effort, but the sight of that girl, the way her screams still echoed in his ears, seemed to empty his mind and to drain his body of strength. As he reached the lower landing, the burly superintendent came striding towards him.

'Are you all right, sir?'

Dawlish drew a deep breath.

'Soon will be. Found her. Get doctor, get ambulance, get everyone out of this place. Quick.' He gave a ghost of a grin and added: 'Please.' At the back of his mind there was fear that this man would argue, but, instead, he felt a firm hand on his arm, and heard reassuring words.

'The doctor's just arrived and I had an ambulance standing by. Just one thing, sir. Shouldn't we search the place?'

'Probably,' Dawlish said. 'What happened to the denizens?'

'The who? Oh. Denizens. Most of them ran.'

'Frightened?'

'Terrified.'

'I beg you, empty the place,' Dawlish said, and then he looked up the staircase and saw Harrison, the girl over his shoulder, coming down. At the same moment the superintendent gave an order in a stentorian, authoritative voice which held no sign of panic.

'Everyone – out. Simpson – Evans – make sure everyone hears. Use the walkie-talkie. Everyone – *out*.'

Harrison staggered at the bottom step and the superintendent went forward and took the girl, without a word. He cradled her in his arms as he went down to the main hall. Two detectives were half-carrying and half-dragging the man whom Dawlish had kicked, the second man was handcuffed to a detective.

'For God's sake get out,' he gasped. 'Get out. The place will go up!'

Dawlish heard. The policemen were already streaming for all the exits, the superintendent and Harrison were at the front door which was wide open. Dawlish was halfway down the stairs. It seemed as if he had leaden weights at his feet and he couldn't hurry. Men pushed past him. The burly superintendent went out at the double and Harrison followed. 'Hurry, sir!' a man shouted in Dawlish's ear, and instead of running past he gripped Dawlish's arm. A draught of cold night air swept in and made Dawlish shiver. Suddenly he was moving fast, through the front doorway, seeing the mass of men lit up in the headlights of cars; an ambulance at the drive entrance, a fire engine in the roadway.

He was halfway along the drive when the explosion came. A vivid flash, a great roar of sound and then a blast which lifted him off his feet and hurled him into the air.

13   Fireworks

Dawlish did not lose consciousness.

He had his wits about him enough to hunch his shoulders and turn his left side towards the ground. He was aware of more explosions, blasts of hot air, flashes which lit up the whole of the area and blazed high into the sky. He saw the grass beneath him and, beyond, a flower-bed. He struck the flower-bed and lay still. His shoulder and arm hurt a little, but not enough to worry about. There was a confusion of sounds and light in his mind. He felt as if the breath had been knocked out of his body and yet could not lie still. He got up on one knee and then on both, half-sinking in the soft earth.

That was when he realized that he had been flung over a high wall.

He could see the flames coming from the windows of the big house next door but not the ground floor. A man appeared beside him, a little man in a short coat and a muffler.

'You all right?' he asked.

It was ridiculous, in a way, to need the help of so small a man. But soon Dawlish was on his feet, rocking a little, firm enough to see over the wall.

Fire seemed to burst from every window, from holes in the roof, from the doorways and the garage. Each time there was a vivid flash, and the flashes were of many colours – white, red, green, pink, blue: it was like a giant firework display. Suddenly, the roof of The Elms seemed to lift high above the house and another deafening roar came. The little man at the wall ducked beneath it, Dawlish covered his head with his arms. Slates and bricks and mortar were hurtling through the air, the sound of crashing glass came often, tinny sounds as the debris fell on the roofs of cars. A brick thumped into the grass in front of Dawlish, a slate struck the flower-bed and buried itself inches deep, standing on edge.

The flash which followed came near to blinding Dawlish.

A few moments afterwards more explosions came, more 'fireworks' in a vivid succession of glorious colours which lit up the sky. Then shapes appeared. At a window, stuck there as if by accident, was the face of a Mephistopheles, much the same as the one which Dawlish had seen when sitting in the car with Justin Franklin. He saw small fires about this garden and the garden of The Elms; there were dozens of these burning demons' faces, some of them enshrouded in mist. Dozens? Surely there were hundreds!

On the roofs of nearby houses people were standing and watching; at every nearby window others stood gaping at the wonder of the scene: and it *was* wonderful, perhaps the most magnificent show of fireworks ever seen in London except on some great State occasion. How long the display lasted, how long he stayed watching, Dawlish didn't know, but he became aware of men calling orders, and of the ringing of a bell; and then he saw two fire-engines moving into the grounds of The Elms, men running ahead of the engines and already unrolling hoses. Before long the worst would be over; soon they should know how much of the house could be salvaged.

The little man dropped down from the wall.

'Spoilsports,' he declared wistfully. 'Won't see anything like that again in *my* lifetime. Talk about the fire of London! How about coming in for a nip?'

Dawlish thought: Whisky?

'Needn't take long,' the man went on, 'I live here. Saw you coming through the air. There's a goner, I said to myself, what's that old song? "I fly through the air with the greatest of ease, the di-di-da-da on the flying trapeze". And there you were, on my bed of dahlias. Sure you're okay?'

'After the nip you so kindly suggested I'll be like a new man.'

'Come on then,' the little neighbour urged. He led the way to a side door, and on through a kitchen to a big room full of heavy, old-fashioned furniture. On an excessively shiny sideboard stood several bottles. 'Brandy?'

'Please.'

The little man, who had a round face and a snub nose and a pair of deepset and surprisingly sober blue eyes, poured out generously, and handed the glass to Dawlish.

'Down the hatch!' he said cheerfully. 'I was having a quick one when the fun started, if truth were known. Blimey! What a turn-up for the book!'

Warmth and comfort spread through Dawlish as he drank.

'I'm better already. Your *very* good health.'

'In the pink, that's me,' the man declared. 'Fred Dando – you may have heard of me if you're a betting man. Fred Dando the bookie. I wouldn't have given you evens that everything was on the up-and-up at The Elms since old Pop Evans died and the new people took over. Proper polyglot lot, if you ask me. I ain't got no colour or race prejudice, I takes me money from all comers and all kinds, but Chinks and Indians, Japs and Pakkis, is going a bit far. And do I know a German and an Itye when I see one! Called it a nursing home they did, but . . .'

Dawlish finished his drink, feeling the exhaustion of body and mind slowly drain away. The little man could certainly talk. Soon he, Dawlish, would forget

115

much of the episode, but Dando wouldn't. He would probably bore every friend and acquaintance with it for the rest of his life.

'Another nip?' Dando asked him.

'No, that was just right,' Dawlish said. 'But now I must let the others know that I'm still in one piece. 'Could you describe these people?'

'What I can't the missus can, eyes like a hawk she has, and if she happened to miss anything her pa would be able to give the answers. Eighty-one and all there *and* he don't need glasses to read by. You one of them?'

'Them?'

'Cops,' explained Fred Dando succinctly.

'Yes,' Dawlish said.

'Big wheel, I bet,' said Dando. 'I've got a feeling I've seen you before, mister. *Strewth!*' Amazement filled his eyes and his mouth opened into a big round O. '*Strewth!*' he repeated. 'You're that Dawlish, aincha? Crime Haters copper. Blimey! I've really been entertaining a VIP tonight. Wait till I tell the missus. *Sure* you won't have another?'

'Not now, really,' Dawlish said.

Fred Dando saw him to the door of a house which was smaller than The Elms but of the same period, and as Dawlish shook hands and Dando wished him an earnest goodbye, a man turned into the street – and then raised his voice and called to others:

'Here he is! Here's Mr Dawlish.'

'Mr Dawlish,' said Fred Dando in a pleading voice, 'will you fix me a trip round the Black Museum? I've always wanted to see – '

'Yes,' Dawlish promised. 'Just as soon as this case is over.'

He lengthened his stride and went towards the street, which was now bathed in a pink glow from the dying fire. He saw not only the burly superintendent but Gordon Scott hurrying towards him. Obviously they had been alarmed, and if he'd been wide awake he would have sent word much earlier. Without going into detail he said that he had been blown into the next door garden where a neighbour had looked after him.

'And he's got a pretty clear idea of the people who went in and out of The Elms,' Dawlish said. 'He and his family will co-operate with us, and with luck you should get a dozen descriptions.'

He told them all he could; and then he learned what there was to learn.

Lisa Day had been taken to the Mandel Clinic, at Chief Inspector Pence's suggestion. Detective Sergeant Harrison was now with Pence telling him all he could about his association with the girl. (In an aside Scott told him there was no news of the Franklins, and that Mrs Gimble was making a good recovery.)

As far as they could judge, most of the occupants of The Elms had been picked up, but once the fireworks had started the crowd had become so thick that some may have slipped through. Nine detentions had been made including the two 'doctors' who had tortured Lisa.

The Elms had been empty for nearly a year before it had been bought by a man named Cartwright – Russell Cartwright. So far the significance of the name was not known to any of the police. It had been called variously a guest house and a nursing home, and was officially registered as a guest house; a record of its residents had been kept and examined twice by the local police. At least half of the guests had been

117

Orientals, but this was not unusual, and nothing had been known against the place, which was now practically gutted.

The fire was nearly out, although the glow remained.

The police had put up wooden barricades to keep the crowds back, but still had difficulty in controlling them. Some streets had been kept clear but nearby gardens had been invaded, while people still perched precariously on rooftops to watch the firemen who were now damping down the wreckage.

In the grounds only three walls were standing, and one of those was only half of its original height. Police officers were searching among the debris for undamaged or only partly damaged objects from the house. Several wheelbarrows had been pressed into service and from somewhere the local police had obtained a number of metal bins which were being used for the salvage. At least thirty men were in sight, and there would be others at the back.

There were as many firemen.

Dawlish and the superintendent and a local chief inspector drew level with the man in charge; a man who looked like a bronzed giant in the glow from the embers, his steel helmet pushed to the back of his head.

'Glad to meet you, Mr Dawlish. I'm told that but for you this would have been a much greater catastrophe.'

Dawlish shrugged.

'I'm only sorry I didn't gain time to search the house first. What are the salvage possibilities?'

'Next door to nil – apart from what your chaps are picking up. Unless – ' He broke off, and wiped his mouth with the back of his hand before going on. 'Unless there's anything in the cellar. These old houses usually have them. We haven't uncovered the entrance yet, the stuff will have to cool down a bit before we can look further. But when this kind of stuff is stored they usually start with the cellar.'

Dawlish's heart rose.

'And anything there should be intact?'

'Should be,' the bronzed man answered. 'If the heat from the fire here had been going to set it off, we'd know by now. We'll damp the floor down for a couple of hours and make sure there aren't any smouldering patches near the cellar before we open it. You can keep your fingers crossed, sir.'

'Never more tightly,' Dawlish said.

By then, he knew, Fred Dando's family was being questioned and were responding eagerly. The fire chief's 'couple of hours' would probably stretch to three or four, and there was nothing more that he could do here. But there were a great number of things he could do at his office.

It was nearly half past nine – Good lord! He must call Felicity!

'I called her and told her you were all right, sir,' Gordon Scott said. 'And she is out for a few hours – at the Farninghams. She asked me to tell you she wouldn't be home until eleven o'clock or later.'

'Oh,' Dawlish said. 'Good.' If he could get what he wanted to do done by half past eleven, say, he would be home about the same time as Felicity and would even be able to get a reasonable night's sleep. 'Take me to the office, Gordon – and I'll talk to Pence on the way.' He turned to the burly superintendent, aware suddenly that this man who had seemed so unco-operative at first had, by the emergency, become a kind of father figure. 'Superintendent,' he said, 'having you on duty tonight was a godsend. Thank you.'

'Working with you has been a – ' The superintendent began, only to hesitate, shrug his big shoulders and say: 'I don't know the word for it. Privilege is an understatement, Mr Dawlish. The way you went into that house was nothing short of – well, I shan't forget it.'

Dawlish felt a glow of pleasure. Surely it was not vain or conceited to be uplifted by another man's considered approval? He hoped not, for his heart sang.

Sitting back in the front seat of Scott's car, he was able to stretch his aching legs out in comparative comfort (not knowing that Scott had bought this particular model because of its exceptional leg room), and it was a moment or two before he put in a radio telephone call for Pence. Pence never seemed to be off duty; certainly never when he was needed.

'Three things you can start on while I'm on my way,' Dawlish said. 'First – do any of the victims have any connection with Hong Kong, or with General Supplies Limited?'

'I'll get busy,' promised Pence.

'Second – we want all the information we can get about a man named Cartwright – Russell Cartwright.'

'He is one of the chief oriental representatives of General Supplies, sir,' interrupted Pence, without any outward show of smugness that he should have been a step ahead. 'And he is also one of the men for whom Miss Day worked. She handled all his correspondence and general business during the previous periods he was travelling. I took the liberty of asking the City people to send someone to check whether her desk had been forced – and to get anything we can on Cartwright. We might have to wait until morning before the answer comes through.'

Dawlish said: 'What on earth I should do without you, Pence, I do not know! God bless you. Meanwhile, I shall go straight to General Supplies, before coming to the office, and Gordon Scott will be with me. A third thing you might begin to check: is there any association between General Supplies and Sir Justin Franklin? Even the most tenuous association would do.'

'It's not very tenuous, sir,' answered Pence, and this time there was an edge of satisfaction in his voice. 'He is on the board. He was consulted some years ago on general business efficiency and two years ago was invited on to the board. I'm afraid there's still no word about him or his wife, sir.'

14   General Supplies Limited

The tall lamps cast strange shadows in the narrow streets of the City of London. The headlights of Scott's car threw more, and longer. It was like going through a city of the dead. The engine made little sound and few cars were about. Dawlish watched the names of the companies and the banks. Royal Bank of Hong Kong – Bank of Thailand – Bangkok National Bank – Chase Manhattan – Formosa – Bank of India – Bank of Burma – People's Bank of the Chinese Republic. There were insurance companies and trading companies, most but not all from the Far East or with Far Eastern associations.

121

At last the white façade of the modern building which housed General Supplies Limited came into view. Dawlish saw that there were several police cars parked close by as well as two City of London policemen standing at the entrance.

A constable directed Dawlish's car into a space that had been left for it. As the man opened the door for him he asked: 'Any excitements?'

'None I know of, sir.'

'What floor do we go to?'

'Seventh, sir. There's an officer at the lift, he'll take you up.'

Dawlish walked with Scott along the wide foyer-like passage to the middle of three lifts, where another City policeman stood ready.

The lift moved with speed and efficiency, and soon they stepped out into an entrance which was much more brightly lighted. On the wall opposite the lifts was the name *General Supplies Limited* in English, in French and in Chinese or Japanese, Dawlish wasn't sure which. Double doors were wide open and as he went forward a tall man in a dark suit, one side of his face badly marked by a burn scar, came forward. Dawlish recognized him as Chief Inspector Mackinson of the City of London Police. With him were two junior officers and an extremely well-dressed man whose immaculacy went strangely with his agitated manner.

'Good evening, Chief Inspector,' Dawlish began.

'Good evening, sir. This is Mr Tenterden, the general manager here, who has been good enough to assist us.'

'Very good of you, sir,' Dawlish said.

'I'm always glad to help the police, but I *must* know

122

why this is necessary.' Tenterden's face was very pale, and there was the hint of a stammer at every fourth or fifth word. Was there also a hint of fear in his eyes? 'All I have been told is that you need to examine the files in Miss Day's desk, and also the files on the three representatives – trusted representatives – for whom she works. I think, I really think, that I should be told why.'

Mackinson looked stolidly at one point above the man's head.

'And so do I,' said Dawlish warmly. 'No one knew until I arrived, though. May we go to her desk?' He started off, the general manager turning to keep pace with him. 'An attempt was made to murder Miss Day this evening.'

'God bless my soul!'

'And we have reason to believe it was because of information which she obtained quite innocently in the way of business.'

'I simply do not believe it. I do not!' Tenterden was positively trotting to keep pace. 'What possible reason – '

'Miss Day has recently acquired a new boy-friend, who is by chance a police officer,' Dawlish said. 'And while it is only conjecture we think that someone knew this and was afraid she might pass on information which was otherwise confidential.' He paused. 'Ah! Are these the filing cabinets?'

'Y-yes,' stammered Tenterden.

'Have you a key, Mr Tenterden?'

'I – no. The only key is in Miss Day's possession, they all – I mean the representatives for whom she works – also have keys, but here – only Miss Day.'

'Oh well,' said Dawlish philosophically. 'I was about

to say that one of the habits policemen – unconventional policemen such as I in particular – acquire is the habit of forcing locks. I shouldn't think this should be too difficult, should you, Mr Mackinson?'

'This' was a five-drawer steel cabinet with a single lock on the top of the casing. Once this was open then all the drawers would open easily when pulled. It stood by the side of a steel typing desk on which stood a typewriter beneath a grey plastic cover; there was a writing desk at right angles to this: it was obvious that the secretarial staff here worked with all possible facilities.

'Very simple, sir, I should say,' agreed Mackinson. His eyes seemed to be asking: Now what's he up to?

Dawlish took a knife out of his pocket and selected a blade which proved to be a length of very flexible high tension steel. Once this were pushed into the lock the moment would come when there was sufficient pressure for it to press back the barrel inside. Dawlish had often forced a lock of this kind in a few seconds, and now he rested a hand on top of the cabinet and inserted the steel blade.

'No!' cried Tenterden. 'Don't do it. Don't do it!'

Dawlish and Mackinson stood absolutely still, and then, very slowly, Dawlish turned towards Tenterden. He had begun to shake, his mouth working as if he could not control his nerves.

'No,' he muttered. 'Don't force it. Don't!'

'And why not?' asked Dawlish in a voice which was positively silky. The man did not answer.

'And why not?' repeated Dawlish, in a stronger voice.

'It – it would blow up,' Tenterden gasped. 'If the lock is forced the whole cabinet will blow up, there will be a terrible fire. It – it would kill us all.'

The others stood silent.

Somewhere a clock ticked clearly, loudly. From outside a car horn blared, but these were the only sounds except the breathing of the men. Tenterden's face was now an ashen grey; even his lips were colourless.

Slowly, Dawlish held out his hand.

'Then supposing you give me the key,' he said. 'None of us wants to be blown up, do we?'

Tenterden said in a gasping voice: 'No, no.' He put his hand to his pocket and Dawlish watched closely; he might bring out a bunch of keys or he might bring out a gun or a knife. He brought out a key case. His fingers trembled as he unzipped it. Opened, there were at least a dozen keys on the chain. Dawlish watched the unsteady fingers groping until at last the selection was made. 'This is it.'

It could be the right key.

It could be a key which would not work properly and would in fact blow them to Kingdom Come.

Dawlish took all the keys, holding them by the one which Tenterden had indicated. Slowly he turned towards the filing cabinet. Mackinson was obviously as aware as he was of the danger, and on the moment of insertion, he said sharply:

'Let me do that, sir. You're – we need your services more than mine.'

'No, no.' Dawlish smiled at him, then looked at Tenterden. There was no way of telling whether the man's pallor was the result of betraying the secret of the safe, or because of the risk of what might happen once the key was turned.

One of the men said: 'Why not make him open it, sir?'

Dawlish did not answer but pushed the key slowly home and then turned it to the right. There was no movement. When he turned it to the left it moved freely. Now he could hear the heavy breathing of all the men as well as the thumping of his own heart.

There was a click. The lock was back.

Dawlish pulled the top drawer open a few inches; it came without any trouble and he saw the neatly placed folders inside. At last he began to breathe freely, sure that the key had circumvented any explosive device.

'You have a great deal to explain,' he said softly.

'Not here,' Tenterden begged. 'Not here, please – take me to the nearest station, lock me up. I won't be safe until I'm locked up. *Please*. You can look at the papers, you can photograph them, you have what you want, and – and I'll tell you about what I know when I'm safe. But not here, I beg you, not here.'

'I think you'd better take him away,' Dawlish said to Mackinson. 'I would hate anything to happen to him. He –'

Across his words came a sharp crack of sound; and as the crack echoed Tenterden gave a choking cough, and his legs doubled up beneath him. Dawlish felt quite sure that he was dead before he reached the ground. If somebody could shoot Tenterden with such accuracy they could shoot any one of them, and in a vivid reflex movement he crouched behind the filing cabinet, and said sharply: 'Down, all of you.'

But Mackinson ignored the warning.

He had obviously seen where the shot had come from and began to run, shouting: '*Up in the corner. Up in the corner!*' Dawlish glanced up and saw a man standing on what looked like a platform in a corner about three-quarters of the way up the wall. He held

126

an automatic and he was levelling it towards the running detective, who made no attempt to take cover.

The range was too great for the gas pistol. The only thing Dawlish or anyone might do to help was to distract his attention. But before he or either of the men near him moved, one of the constables by the door took his truncheon from his waistband, poised it, and then threw it, rather like an athlete might throw a javelin, at the man on the platform. The truncheon struck the man on the shoulder before he even realized that it was coming, and he dropped the gun.

By then, Mackinson was near the corner, where a flight of iron steps led to a kind of mezzanine floor where there were rows of filing cabinets. Mackinson went up the steps like a streak. The gunman, recovering his balance, kicked out and caught him a glancing blow on the side of the head, but the inspector simply grabbed at his ankle and pulled him off his feet. The steel landing and the staircase boomed and clattered as the two men fell. How Mackinson did it Dawlish did not quite know, but suddenly he saw the two men standing, handcuffed together.

Almost at once there was a bellow from the lift foyer, and Dawlish's relief turned again to sudden anxiety. He reached the foyer as a policeman picked himself up from the floor.

'I was attacked from the stairs, sir. I hope to God the devil didn't get away.'

But the other man, obviously one of two who had come to kill Tenterden, had disappeared.

A pity, thought Dawlish. Never mind, at least they had the man with the gun, and had succeeded in unlocking the safe.

Dawlish walked towards the entrance to the lifts,

meeting Mackinson and his handcuffed prisoner at the open doors.

'Magnificent,' he said warmly to Mackinson.

'I didn't mean this swine to get away,' Mackinson said gruffly, 'only wish we'd got 'em both. Where do you want him?'

'Cannon Row, if you don't mind me having custody,' said Dawlish, for Cannon Row Police Station was close to his offices and outside the precincts of the City of London.

'Welcome,' said Mackinson. 'I'll take him there for you.'

'Thanks,' said Dawlish. 'Meanwhile we'll need an ambulance for Tenterden, and I'd like an explosive expert to check those files before we take the documents out for examination and photographing.'

'Bomb-disposal unit, I'd say,' suggested Mackinson.

Dawlish, looking at him, wondered what particular act of courage had earned him the scar that lay like an insignia across his face.

'I'll stay here until the experts arrive,' Dawlish said, 'and again – magnificent.'

Mackinson went downstairs with his prisoner and one of his own men, while Dawlish sat on a corner of Lisa Day's desk and tried the telephone. It was connected with the exchange and he called his office. Pence answered instantly, listened, then said: 'I'll see to it all, sir,' and rang off. Replacing the receiver, Dawlish looked up as Gordon Scott and another of the City of London men approached him.

'Anything?' asked Dawlish.

Gordon shook his head.

'We've checked and the three floors are empty. I

shouldn't think we'd have any more trouble here to-night, sir.'

'No,' Dawlish said. 'Please God.'

He sat absolutely still, thoughts first drifting, then racing through his head. *Was* it possible that all the answers were somewhere in these offices? *Was* it possible that Justin Franklin had been even remotely involved in the dreadful treatment of his own wife? Was Hong Kong the key to what had been going on? Would these files and Lisa Day be able to yield up vital secrets?

There were other questions, and one above all others tore at him.

Were there other places like The Elms?

The attacks on the women – *why women*? – had taken place in so many countries. Would the disaster to the group in England mean that action would start more quickly in other countries?

What action? he almost groaned. What were they planning to do?

That was the question tearing at his heart and mind when a lieutenant, a sergeant, and a private of a bomb-disposal unit arrived to check the files.

15   Lisa Day Talks

Within twenty minutes the young lieutenant and his sergeant had found the secret of the file. A highly powerful explosive was concealed in false sides and would be blown up by an electric short circuit if the cabinet were forced. Only after it had been removed were the files lifted out of the drawers. The two top ones contained papers, orders copies of letters written by or to Lisa Day. The others were filled with the correspondence of Russell Cartwright, and the two other representatives of General Supplies Limited who operated in the Far and Middle East. One was a Lionel Tyge; the other, a Benjamin Abbott. All the correspondence appeared to be straightforward business. It was, of course, possible that there was some kind of code.

Dawlish talked by telephone to the Assistant Commissioner.

'Yes, I've had a report, Pat. A wonderful job at The Elms. . . . Yes, we'll get some cypher experts at the papers immediately, the Ministry of Defence or the Foreign Office will help. . . . Yes,' he replied to another question, 'we need to make a thorough examination of the main managerial offices of General Supplies, and by George yes, you'd better have your explosive experts there to check. . . . I'll arrange it with the chairman of the company. We need full access to all records. It will take a little time, of course.'

'Not too much time, please,' Dawlish begged. 'Can you send enough men over – I've twice as much work on as my chaps can handle.'

'I'll see to it,' the AC said. 'What about the girl, Lisa Day? Has she talked yet?'

'I doubt it – I'm not sure when she'll be able to,' Dawlish said. 'But I'm going over to see her at Mandel's now.'

'Pat,' the AC said, in what could be taken as a forbidding tone.

'Sir?'

'I don't want you to overdo it. Why don't you go home and get a good night's sleep? The pressure may be even greater in the morning.'

'By then I may be flying to Hong Kong,' Dawlish told him. 'I'm with you in spirit but I won't be able to relax until I know what the girl has to say. Have you any news of the Franklins?'

'None at all,' the AC replied.

Dawlish rang off, very thoughtfully. He sat at his desk, alone, for perhaps ten minutes, and knew that the other man was right: he needed relaxation, he needed sleep; he could not concentrate enough. His own car was in the courtyard here but he had Pence send a driver; he did not trust himself to drive.

Everything that had happened seemed to move chaotically round in his mind.

There was the almost incredible fact that he had only made as much progress as he had because a Scotland Yard detective had fallen in love with a girl at General Supplies. It was the kind of thing one would not think up in one's wildest fancies, but it had happened – unless, of course, Lisa Day had deliberately set out to attract Harrison because something had aroused her suspicions.

'One doesn't have to *have* a rational explanation of everything,' he muttered to himself. What was rational about Franklin taking his wife away from the Mandel Clinic, the one place where she might get help? Why had Franklin got in touch with him? By sheer chance, or by a process of reasoning, or because he wanted police action but could not say so openly?

It made sense that if he were involved in the crimes and if his own wife had become a victim he would

131

hate everyone involved but – all he had done was run away and spirit Ursula away at the same time.

Why? Dawlish demanded of himself as the car sped along to the Mandel Clinic.

The night duty nurse whom he had seen the night before opened the door, and did not seem at all surprised to see him.

'Dr Mandel was sure you would come,' she said. 'He is with Miss Day now, and the news is good.'

'How good?' demanded Dawlish eagerly.

'She has responded very well to treatment, and Dr Mandel feels sure that he will be able to induce amnesia so that she will forget what has happened,' the nurse said. Her eyes twinkled. 'But he felt sure you would like to talk to her first!'

She took him into the waiting-room, vividly reminiscent of the time he had spent there only a few short hours ago. He did not have to wait more than three or four minutes before Mandel came in.

He was smiling, a startling difference to the last time Dawlish had seen him.

'I am glad for once to have good news for you,' he said as they shook hands, '*very* good news, in fact! Not only is the injury to Lisa Day slight, there is a marked improvement in the condition of Mrs Gimble.'

If only he had been able to say: Lady Franklin.

'I have been attempting a new technique,' Mandel went on, leading the way along the carpeted passage, 'but as with all untried techniques in neuro-surgery and the therapeutic treatment of brain damage, great care has to be used in the beginning. Great care!' he repeated. 'Everything has to be done with the utmost caution. I sometimes wonder if others realize the burden of responsibility that rests on those dealing with

132

the human mind.' He stopped with his hand on the door of one of the rooms. 'But one day there will even be brain transplants!'

He tapped at the door and almost at once opened it and went in.

Lisa Day, whom Dawlish had seen in conditions of such distress and horror, was lying back on a nest of pillows. She wore a bedjacket of soft angora wool, her hair had been brushed and groomed, and her lips were faintly touched with pink. The contrast with the woman whom he had seen strapped to the bed was astonishing.

She looked at Mandel with obvious trust, and then up at Dawlish as if to ask: Who is this man?

'I promised you would soon see Mr Dawlish,' Mandel said in his gentle voice.

She caught her breath.

For a moment Dawlish did not understand her reaction, nor her weakness, for tears welled up in her eyes as she stared at him. Then she held out her hands, both hands, and when he went forward and took them she held his own very tightly.

'Bob told me what happened,' she said. 'It – it is so empty to say "thank you".'

'But often very rewarding,' Dawlish replied.

She opened her mouth to speak again, hesitated, then gave a little laugh. Tears spilled over the edge of her eyes and rolled down her cheeks.

'Bob worships you,' she said.

Dawlish forced a smile.

'Bob hardly knows me.'

'He knows everything it's possible to know about the Crime Haters. He – '

'Let's think about Bob later,' Dawlish said. He leaned forward and kissed her forehead, and then released his hands, dug into his pocket and took out an unfolded handkerchief. 'My wife always prefers to use this herself,' he said. 'She tells me I make a hopeless mess of her make-up!'

Lisa gave another little laugh as she dabbed gently at her cheeks.

'Thank you.'

'Lisa.' Dawlish said, 'I hate to question you now but it's very important for us to know what questions these men asked you, what they wanted to find out.'

'Talking about it doesn't worry me,' she assured him. 'I can't remember every detail but I can remember what they were doing all the time. They thought I was giving information to Bob, spying on them. They didn't believe that we'd met by chance and that I – Promise you won't tell Bob.'

'I promise.'

'They simply wouldn't believe that I love him,' she said.

Dawlish patted her shoulder.

'That's a thing for you to tell him,' he said, and after a pause went on: 'Were there any specific questions, about any people or documents or anything of the kind?'

'No,' she said. 'They really thought I was spying on them. When they realized I was telling the truth they – they took a hypodermic syringe out of a cabinet, and said something about giving me what they'd given the others. I couldn't see their faces, but their voices were – demoniac.'

Dawlish stared down at her very intently. After a few moments he said:

'Lisa, you were very lucky.'

'I – I know. And you – '

'A great many women have been through the ordeal you suffered, and many were left seriously ill. Some – as Dr Mandel will tell you – will never really be themselves again. After a while something in their brains snapped. It could not be more vital for me to know exactly what is in your mind, everything you can possibly tell me.'

'I know,' she said. 'Bob – Bob told me about the burning masks, and – ' She swallowed hard before going on in a stronger voice: 'Russell Cartwright brought some from Hong Kong. Lionel Tyge brought some from Singapore and Ben Abbott brought some from Bangkok. They were uncanny little things. They – they all three sent small parcels to the office. I should have sent them on to The Elms, but I opened them by mistake. A new office girl had actually started to open them, and I took them from her to repack. I couldn't help seeing.'

'And?' urged Dawlish.

'They contained some of these little masks.'

'Was anything else with them?'

'No.'

'Did you ever have to send such parcels to anyone else?'

'No,' she said. 'As I understood it these were samples which went to The Elms for test and analysis, and they came by air. The bulk supplies went to other warehouses in England and in Europe.' She was looking very puzzled. 'The masks made me shudder, I just didn't like them, but – '

'Lisa,' interrupted Dawlish. 'Wasn't it strange that all three should reach you at the same time from three different places?'

'Oh, no,' she answered. 'It was quite usual. I think

135

a special messenger brought them and they certainly arrived on the same aircraft by air freight. Some freight planes stop at each of the places and it would be a natural progression – Hong Kong, Singapore, Bangkok. There was nothing strange about it.'

'Is there a list of the places where the larger consignments went to?' asked Dawlish.

'Of course – these and hundreds of other different things. You see, General Supplies often acted as agents. They didn't buy and sell but arranged the consignments of goods from manufacturer direct to customer, cutting out a lot of middleman's profits. They received a commission of which half went to the company, half to the individual agent and representative. I simply kept a record of the transactions of these three, Russell Cartwright, Lionel – '

'I know the names,' Dawlish said. 'And I've been able to get permission to open the filing cabinets.'

'Don't open them without a key,' warned Lisa. 'They give off tear gas and I'm told it's a *very* effective antiburglar device!' It did not appear to occur to her that the 'tear gas' could be a highly destructive explosive. 'I hate to think that any one of the three is doing anything unlawful, Mr Dawlish.'

'It's possible they are just being used,' Dawlish said. 'Who else deals with the papers in your files?'

'No one. I was directly responsible to the general manager.'

'Mr Tenterden?'

'Yes.' Lisa frowned for a moment and then closed her eyes. 'He seldom wanted to see anything, just the dates of consignments of certain things. I – I don't really remember which ones but – *are* you going to examine the files?'

Her eyes were brighter now but not with tears; a kind of glassy brightness which warned him that she was getting over-tired. He heard Mandel stir beside him, and so absorbed had he been in all Lisa had told him that he had forgotten the surgeon had been in the room all the time.

'When Mr Tenterden had seen a consignment note or any document I always marked it in a corner with a capital T in red – so that I would know he'd seen it. Absolutely no one else was allowed access. Why even –' She stifled a yawn, and during the pause Mandel stepped forward and said:

'No more, Mr Dawlish, please.'

'No,' agreed Dawlish. 'Just this one thing. What were you going to say, Lisa?'

'Just that even the directors weren't allowed access. Sir Justin Franklin is on the board and he was extremely curious about the three special agents, as he called them, but he had no authority from Mr Tenterden, so I couldn't allow him to see a thing.' She laughed and yawned at the same time. 'He wasn't very pleased with me!'

'I could not be more pleased with you,' said Dawlish, and he bent down and kissed her forehead. 'Good night. I'll make sure Bob comes and sees you in the morning.'

He drew back, and Mandel raised a hand to the girl, wished her good night and, as a nurse came in, obviously in answer to a summons, he said: 'Miss Day is ready to settle down for the night now, nurse. Two tablets and a small glass of warm milk. If she should be restless, let me know.'

'Very good, Doctor.'

Dawlish was already outside in the passage, aware

of what was being said but not thinking about it. He was thinking only about the fact that Franklin had wanted access to those papers. He should have asked Lisa when that had happened, but he couldn't go back now. She had stood up to the questioning remarkably well, but anything more might delay her recovery. Mandel joined him, and led the way along the passage, saying only: 'She will be perfectly all right, she has a particularly strong character.' A moment later he asked: 'Would you like to see Mrs Gimble now?'

'May I?'

'For a moment, yes,' said Mandel, and he opened a door on the right, on to another room almost identical with the one they had just left.

Mrs Gimble was asleep, and it seemed to be a natural sleep.

'She looks very peaceful,' Dawlish said.

'I believe she is at peace,' replied Mandel gravely, 'but such cases are very precarious and should be treated at once. I am greatly worried over Lady Franklin. Is there any way at all in which you can persuade her husband to bring her back?'

16   Cure?

Dawlish thought: Why did he take her away?

He looked at the peacefully sleeping woman and he remembered Lisa as she was now and as she had been only a few hours before: in terror and on the edge of madness.

He remembered other women whom he had seen hours and even days after their ordeal, and the recollection touched him with horror.

If there *was* a cure –

Finding why this was happening was vital, finding who was behind it even more important, and both objectives seemed nearer than they had been a few hours before.

'If – God forbid – there should be new victims, are you sure you can save them?' he asked.

'As sure as any doctor can be of anything,' answered Mandel. 'Some exceptions – failures – will be inevitable. Some recoveries will be more complete than others, some will take longer, but I am quite sure that I have made a breakthrough. It is not possible to explain to you in scientific terms, but it is really very simple for the intelligent layman to understand. There are two problems. One is the actual brain damage caused largely by electrolosis and shocks to the brain cells, drugs and electricity being used together. The effect is to fuse some cells which work perfectly as individuals but when fused become scrambled – confused. They then refuse to work, and the mind atrophies. In extreme cases there is virtually no mind left at all, the effect being identical with that of an illness which starves the brain of blood and oxygen. Do you understand?'

Dawlish nodded.

'The second problem deals with that part of the brain which carries memory. When memory of the pain and all that happened floods back when there is still only partial recovery, it causes a fear which has a paralytic effect on the brain and throws the patient back to complete unawareness of life.'

139

'So to cure one without the other wouldn't be much help,' Dawlish observed.

'You are quite right. However the first problem is comparatively simple. Cures can be achieved with electro-physiotherapy and drugs. The damage is *not* irreparable in itself. The second has been the worst problem: to create a state of amnesia in the mind without causing injury to the other brain cells; to black out all recollection of the ordeal. And this, I am now sure, can be achieved by drugs and physiotherapy, applied in a way which I am positive will stand any test.'

'And you're trying it on Mrs Gimble?'

'Yes.'

'Can you explain it to other neuro-surgeons so that they can apply the treatment to their patients?' asked Dawlish.

For a moment, Mandel hesitated. It was the first time Dawlish had felt the slightest disappointment in the man, for the hesitancy could so easily imply that he wanted to keep the discovery to himself. It was no doubt the result of lifelong research, but if anything belonged to humanity, surely this did.

To his surprise, Mandel smiled, very charmingly.

'You are doing me an injustice, Mr Dawlish.'

'Was I as obvious as that?'

'You are very tired, and although you are adept at hiding your feelings, this time the disappointment showed clearly.' Mandel spread his hands. 'Perhaps I am too perceptive or too imaginative! I was not expressing any unwillingness to share this newly acquired technique, but doubt as to whether it could easily be – or even effectively be – explained by letter or even by telephone. Telephone would perhaps be possible but it might mean hours on the subject with

140

each of perhaps a hundred doctors. *At least* a hundred. I really don't see how I can pass on the technique in time to be of immediate help in this crisis.'

Silence followed his words.

Silence while Mrs Gimble lay sleeping so peacefully, and Mandel stood so obviously distressed, and Dawlish stared at and virtually through him. Everything he said was right, and yet there must be a simple answer. Frowning as the idea began to form in his mind, he asked slowly:

'Supposing you could get them all together in one place – '

'Here in London do you mean?'

'London or some even more central spot. Could you then pass on the technique?'

Mandel's frown began to clear, and he clasped his hands together in deep thought. There was a minute or two of silence, and then he said abruptly:

'Could you arrange this?'

'I think so.'

'Then I think, I am almost sure, it could be done.' He moved forward and gripped Dawlish's arm tightly. 'Can you be *sure*? I would have to prepare a paper and have it circulated to the doctors who attended, and that will take time, while I shall have to be away from the clinic for at least a week. But I can and will do both if you can promise me you can arrange such a conference.'

Dawlish said quietly: 'How soon can you be ready?'

'I shall need two days,' declared Mandel. 'At least two clear days. I have an associate here who will be able to take care of the present patients and any new ones who may be brought in. Mr Dawlish, this will be a revolution in neuro-surgery and the treatment of

141

brain damage, and usually it would take months, even years, to persuade other doctors and surgeons of its effectiveness. This way it may be possible to convince them in a matter of *days*. For they may try it on cases they have given up as hopeless, and if they get any results there...'

His eyes saw a vision as he talked on.

Dawlish stepped into the lift that was to carry him up to his flat at half past twelve. It was an hour later than he had hoped, but he had thought it best to go to his own office first and send to other police forces a teletype report of his discussion with Mandel and the request:

Recommend such a convention or conference of neuro-surgeons concerned with the present investigations be arranged. Stop. Suggest also all international Police Delegates who can possibly attend be there. Stop. Reply urgently awaited.

This had gone out, and Gordon Scott, back at the office, was already making tentative arrangements for the convention. It was possible that some could not attend but he felt sure there would be a fair response.

The search at General Supplies had yielded no results so far, except the names of the warehouses to which consignments of the special goods from Hong Kong had been sent. Scott was eager to start raiding, Pence more cautious.

'After what happened at The Elms they'll be especially careful,' he said. 'I'd make sure we know them all, and have them watched. If any start to panic they can be stopped. If they don't, then we can arrange for simultaneous raids all over Europe. That way no factory chief can warn another.'

'I suppose you're right,' Scott had said, grudgingly.

He stepped out into the foyer. The man on duty there was smoking but put a hand smartly down by his side as if by so doing he could hide both smoke and cigarette and at the same time the odour of tobacco.

'Good evening, sir! Mrs Dawlish hasn't been back for long.'

'That's good,' Dawlish said, his heart lifting.

He heard her the moment he opened the door, coming along the passage from the bedroom. She was already in housecoat and slippers, her hair brushed for the night. Her face lit up at the sight of him, and he kicked the door closed with his heel as she drew level and gave her a hug which squeezed the breath out of her.

'My!' she exclaimed. 'What a guilty conscience you must have!'

'Spend all my evenings with attractive young women,' Dawlish said, and kissed her. 'If they're lucky one of them might grow up to be half as nice as you.'

'Compliments, too. Hungry?'

'I suppose I am.'

'Omelette? Cold ham? Tea, coffee, beer?'

'Omelette, maybe some cold ham to help it down. Coffee.' He gave her a lighter hug. 'Sweetheart, I think we're making progress.'

'*And* you're alive,' Felicity said.

'Who's been talking?' demanded Dawlish suspiciously.

'You wash, I'll cook, we'll talk,' replied Felicity, as she went on to the kitchen. He turned into the bathroom. Five minutes later, refreshed by a quick shower,

143

clad in a towelling dressing-gown of many colours, he followed her. Felicity was just lifting the omelette from the pan. At the table he found bread and butter, and some gorgeous-looking ham. The bread was crusty and looked homemade.

'Tess Farningham made it,' Felicity said, 'and that is real farmhouse butter.' She brought the omelette over, poured coffee for herself and sat opposite him. 'You're tired out,' she announced.

'Don't tell me,' Dawlish said. 'I know. The Assistant Commissioner of the Metropolitan Police telephoned you. "Fel old girl", he said, "I don't want to alarm you but Pat is overdoing it. He was nearly blown into little pieces tonight rescuing a beauteous damsel – " '

'He said *nothing* about a beauteous damsel!'

'Well, that shows the poor chap has some tact after all. Nevertheless, the next bit runs: "The old boy's definitely overdoing it. If you have any influence over him, get him to take a pill that will make him sleep for at least eight hours." *Mmm-mmm*! The best omelette I've tasted in years. Well, didn't he?'

Felicity nodded, and there was love and devotion in her smile as she replied:

'Well, more or less.'

'Sweetheart, you can scrub it. I don't need any pill to make me sleep. I've done everything I possibly can, and about the only thing that would make me stir for the next twenty-four hours is news of the Franklins. I would stay up all night if I could find out where to get them.' He held his knife over the ham, then carved. He ate the ham with bread on which he spread the homemade butter generously, and then drank a cup of coffee. He was in the middle of this, and of telling Felicity about Mandel's breakthrough, when he

144

yawned. Suddenly he felt so overwhelmingly tired that he could hardly hold his cup.

Felicity actually led him to bed.

He was asleep before she had brushed her teeth. She stood for a few moments looking down on him. The only light was on her side of the bed and it cast a pale shadow over his face. The strength in that face, overlaid now by utter exhaustion, touched her. She had never known him as a boy. He had been in his middle twenties when they had met during the Second World War. She could remember now the shock with which she had learned that he spent much of his time parachuting behind enemy lines, helping stranded pilots and escaped prisoners out of occupied Europe; and, later, organizing the French Resistance.

Where did his courage come from?

And his reserves of strength?

She did not bend down and kiss him, there was just the chance that it would wake him. She did switch off the bell of the telephone which rang in this room; one of Dawlish's men, outside, would intercept any calls. She lay down at last, and was awake for some time, listening to his deep and even breathing.

The AC had told her a great deal of what had happened. Dear old Pence had told her more. She knew how lucky he was to be alive. She knew how elated he was by Dr Mandel's breakthrough. She longed for the affair to end, because once it was over there would at least be a brief respite.

She was wondering if she could beguile him into letting her go with him on his next adventure, when she dropped off to sleep.

Most of London slept.

But the police, including those in Dawlish's division,

worked on, in a dogged effort to locate and to put cordons around the warehouses which were named in the files. Pence and three of his assistants were also busy, keeping in close touch with those farther afield. There was not a single false move.

Pence slept in a room near the office while his night staff received and sorted messages from members of the Crime Haters all over the world. More and more evidence was forthcoming about the association of women victims from Hong Kong. Some had lived there with the British Armed Forces, some had been wives and daughters of police officers who had for years kept the Hong Kong Police Force at the highest state of efficiency. Some had relatives there. Three, as far as was yet known, had only visited the colony as tourists. Others – and this was the largest single group – worked for firms which had business with the island and its mainland counterpart, Kowloon.

The shipments of fireworks came from individuals, but, mainly, from one small company known as Wen Li Sing and Sons. Wen Li Sing was an old man who had prospered by trading with the great water cities of the island – with the hundreds of thousands who lived on junks or smaller boats, some even on sampans. The company dealt in general merchandise, not only that which was manufactured in Hong Kong. Some goods – mostly antiques of extreme value – were smuggled across the frontier north of Kowloon but other Chinese products and raw materials were shipped to the west by Wen Li Sing and Sons.

They represented General Supplies Limited of London.

They dealt in fireworks, masks, a great variety of Chinese ornamental goods, china, radios, televisions and

146

toys. They were extremely prosperous and in Hong Kong they had an irreproachable reputation.

Their main workshops and warehouses were on Kowloon, not far from the border of China, surrounded with rice fields and other plantations. Their small factories and warehouses were dotted throughout the mainland and the island. Thousands of Hong Kong Chinese families made parts for their different goods, made and painted the masks, made the fireworks, which were part of China's, and so of Hong Kong's, tradition.

Dawlish dreamt of fireworks; dreamt of the roof being lifted off The Elms and the magnificent display which had followed. He dreamt of the faces of demons, and of the fire which surrounded them – the fires as of hell and the mist which could have represented the smoke from hell. He woke suddenly, and for a moment stared at the window, which he was facing, the dressing-table, the familiar bedroom. He stayed absolutely still for a few seconds, a blank expression in his eyes. Then a thought flashed through his mind and he said with great clarity:

'To prevent them from remembering, of course.'

Felicity, her back to him, stirred but did not speak.

'To prevent them from remembering, and so to prevent them from talking,' Dawlish said with the same clarity. 'Motive number one.'

Felicity said sleepily: 'Do you want something?'

'More sense,' Dawlish said. 'Whoever was responsible for these diabolical happenings did not want to kill but did want to make sure that the victims (a) could not remember what had happened to them and so could not give their torturers away and (b) could not tell anyone what they remembered about Hong Kong.'

147

'You're going to Hong Kong?' cried Felicity. 'This morning?'

'I don't know yet,' Dawlish replied. 'It's nearly daylight so it must be getting late. Why don't you stay in bed for an extra hour, sweet? I'll have breakfast at the office.' As he spoke he pushed the bedclothes back, and Felicity knew that this would be one of those mornings when his mind would be anywhere but on her; and when it would be useless to talk about going with him, whether to Hong Kong or Africa.

When Dawlish looked in, a quarter of an hour later, she seemed to be asleep. He blew her a kiss from the door, and as he did so, the telephone bell rang. He was within arm's reach of an extension and flung out a hand and snatched it up; he might still be in time to prevent the bell from waking Felicity.

'Dawlish,' he said.

'This is Master Relativity,' said a voice that was unmistakably Franklin's. 'Where can we meet, in private?'

17   Rendezvous

For a few seconds Dawlish did not answer. A clock in the hall struck nine; it was later than he realized. He believed he could hear Franklin's breathing, but could not be sure.

At last Dawlish said: 'The Mandel Clinic, with your wife?'

'Try again.'

'Master Relativity,' Dawlish said solemnly, 'every

148

policeman in London and a very large number in the rest of the world are on the look-out for you. You can stay in hiding for a few hours, even for a few days, but no longer.'

'A few days will be enough,' Franklin said. 'Name a meeting place, Pat.' There was a note of pleading in his voice. 'Don't spoil it now.'

'Spoil what?'

'You've performed all your miracles, blown up a house, discovered at least a part of what is going on, uncovered the secret of General Supplies and its manager, Paul Tenterden, and a lot about the Far Eastern representatives as well as Wen Li Sing, Russell Cartwright, Lionel Tyge and Benjamin Abbott. You're halfway there but you could still lose.'

'Your wife can still lose her mind, if she isn't returned to the Mandel Clinic.'

'Dawlish, don't be a bloody fool! Mandel's place is as vulnerable as The Elms was, and – but never mind that. I've got Ursula where she's comfortable and can't come to any harm, and thank God she can't remember what happened. You know and I know that this affair is far too big for us to be – to be influenced by the fate of individuals, whoever they are. You're halfway to the solution. I can tell you the other half, but only if we can meet in secret – and I *mean* secret.' There was an instant's pause before Franklin went on: 'Give it some hard thought. I'll call your office at twelve o'clock.'

Dawlish replaced the receiver very slowly. If one thing was certain, Franklin had not talked like a man with a heavy weight on his conscience – though that wasn't significant. What he had shown was the arrogance which had been characteristic of him as a boy; anger at not getting his own way.

Unless he were traced, there should be a call from him in three hours. During those hours Dawlish would have time to think. Think! He grinned to himself: there would probably be no time at all for conscious thinking, but his subconscious would grab the problem and an answer would come: to go, or not to go.

He peeped in at Felicity; she was still fast asleep.

He went out, and this time a different man was on duty in the lift foyer. He sprang to attention at once.

'Good morning, sir!' He pressed for the lift.

'Morning. All quiet on the western front?'

'Quiet as a dormouse since seven, sir, when I came on duty.'

'May it long remain so,' said Dawlish as the lift arrived and the doors opened and he stepped inside.

In the mornings the lift would, normally, stop at several floors to let out the workers, but this morning it went straight down. Two uniformed policemen and one of his own division were in the downstairs foyer, and he could see his own car parked close by the entrance, a police car with a driver just behind it. He was getting very great care and consideration this morning. There was a series of 'greetings' before he said:

'I'll walk, but will you keep close behind me? And could someone park my car?'

'Yes, sir.'

'Will do, sir.'

He walked into a rarely beautiful November morning. The sun was rising above the tops of the buildings on the South Bank of the Thames, into a clear, pale sky. The air was crisp but not bitingly cold. A few leaves of rich reds and browns fluttered down from

150

nearby trees. He crossed the road, looking across at the Abbey and ahead to Parliament Square, seeing in the far distance Nelson's head and shoulders bathed in gold.

It was years since there had been such a morning.

Big Ben began to strike; the quarter, the half past nine. He was tempted to walk along Whitehall, but resisted; he did walk fifty yards on to Westminster Bridge, doubtless to the consternation of his driver who had been forced to go round Parliament Square and would lose sight of him here. He looked along the terrace of the House of Commons and on to the calm movement of the river.

It was almost unearthly in its beauty.

Slowly, very slowly, his mood changed, and he saw a red glow of a different kind; the glow of the burning house; the great explosions and the flashes.

Why?

He turned back to the traffic lights which faced the embankment.

He could understand the way the victims had been treated, now; to kill their minds and so their memories *without killing* their bodies. Had even one of them been murdered in the beginning it would have started a hue and cry, whereas dozens had been tortured and then their minds killed –

Not killed, thanks to Mandel.

He passed the driver, raised a hand and turned into the old building.

Why the fireworks? Why the intense secrecy? What was being plotted under cover of demoniac action?

He missed a step.

Fireworks? Had the conflagration at The Elms really been caused by fireworks or by something much more deadly? Some fireworks were fairly powerful, but that fire had taken a hold so viciously that there had been no chance of saving –

Good lord!

That house had been made of solid Victorian brick, and the wood would have been old and tough – the roof put on with a skill in workmanship which had lasted for a century and should have lasted for another. But the roof had been lifted off in one enormous blast, and the fire had been so fierce that the only things left had been a few crumbling walls, and charred and smouldering rubble.

Fireworks? He gave a short, mirthless laugh.

Only the most advanced explosive with instant combustion fuses could have caused it. Fireworks be damned! Now his heart was beginning to race and he went up in the lift impatiently and strode along to his office. He couldn't expect Pence and Gordon Scott to be in yet, they –

There was Pence, solid as a Buddha, and Gordon Scott, and Sergeant Robert Harrison, all bending towards the world map, so intently that only Harrison noticed the door open. He looked round, then sprang to attention.

'Sir!'

'Doesn't anyone sleep around here?' demanded Dawlish.

The others turned, and there was no doubt of the eagerness in their eyes; in Harrison's, too. Harrison was a good-looking chap, no doubt about that.

'Well, what's new?' demanded Dawlish.

'In all, we know of at least three places in each major European city and one cache in many smaller European cities where the goods have been sent,' Pence answered. 'We haven't yet had an answer from Helsinki or from Milan, but all the others are in.'

'And watched and surrounded?' Dawlish said.

'And watched and surrounded.'

'What about the cellar at The Elms – has anyone been able to force a way in there yet?'

'Living quarters, sir,' answered Pence.

'*What*?'

'Just living quarters for up to twenty or thirty people – mostly men,' Pence answered in more detail. 'The place has been thoroughly searched and nothing found of any significance. There were two escape tunnels, one with an exit in the shrubbery in the garden next door – Fred Dando's garden – and one in the garden immediately behind The Elms. Very cleverly camouflaged, sir, and in places that wouldn't easily be noticed. But we've got something else, sir.'

'What?' Dawlish almost barked.

'The names of agencies of General Supplies and Wen Li Sing's in most other countries in the world, sir. These were found after a search of Mr Tenterden's offices in General Supplies. And we're beginning to get reports that warehouses are being located, watched and surrounded in New York, Buenos Aires, several other cities, Pekin and – well, they're coming in so fast it will soon be a question of you name it, we'll have it. But – ' He broke off, to draw a broad hand across his forehead, then went on: 'Not a single idea why, sir. Not a single idea of any kind.'

Gordon Scott, an old friend who had fought with him since the early days of the Crime Haters; Pence, who had been here only a year; Harrison, who somehow 'belonged' even though he had not been assigned to the Branch, all stared at him as if they regarded him as an oracle from whose mouth an answer to the whole problem was to be expected. They did not question him, even with their eyes, but simply waited in obvious anticipation.

He said: 'Not fireworks.'

None of them responded.

'Much too powerful and damaging for fireworks. If that amount of explosive had been concentrated in one spot instead of spread all over the house, it would have been enough to blow up – '

'Buckingham Palace!' Harrison suggested.

'The Houses of Parliament,' Pence said, soberly.

'Any large building – offices or factory or whatever,' declared Gordon Scott.

'Yes. And there are concentrations of the explosives in the guise of fireworks in hundreds of towns and cities, including all the world's major cities,' Dawlish went on. He spoke as if he were indeed an oracle, the words spoken through him. Both Pence and Scott had seen him like this before, but to Harrison it was a new experience; a revelation. 'So key places in any such cities could easily be blown up.'

No one spoke, but Harrison gave a half-sigh, half-snort.

'Another fact,' Dawlish went on. 'No one would do what these people have done to the women for the sake of it. Organized sadism – I don't believe it. Individual cases, yes. Coincidental cases, yes – when a man working on one of the victims loses all self-control and reveals himself as a natural sadist, yes. But not hundreds of cases.'

Still no one spoke; it was as if they were afraid of breaking a spell.

'So, the purpose of the torture was presumably al-

ways the same as the purpose with Lisa Day, last night.
They wanted information from her. They wanted above
all to find out whether she had talked to Harrison or to
anybody about her work, and it is obvious that they
wanted to find out whether she knew what was going
on. She didn't. Once convinced of that, the indications
are that they were going to treat her as they had
treated the others. I heard them say so. The others had
been treated by electrolosis and drugs so as to kill or
so damage certain brain cells that the victims would
have no recollection of what had happened, could never
name the individuals who had tortured them.'

Harrison drew in a hissing breath.

'So, it could only be for a reason of great and over-
riding importance,' Dawlish went on. 'One might ask,
why didn't they kill the victims? But murder has
always been regarded as the cardinal crime, the evidence of a dead body more conclusive than a broken
mind. It was not until a comparatively short time ago
that we began to realize what hideous crimes were being
committed, and the central or major crime was no doubt
well on its way in the planning stages by then.'

Dawlish paused, and it was so quiet that the different
level of breathing of all three men could be distin-
guished. Very slowly, as if the thought as well as the
words were being forced out of him, he went on:

'Recently there has been a change in tactics: the ab-
solute secrecy has ended, overt attempts to frighten me,
and Franklin, or both of us, have been made. This may
mean that we are fast approaching a climax. After the
raid on General Supplies Head Offices last night and
the destruction of The Elms, the climax may come
much sooner than we expect and the perpetrators
intended.

155

'It *must* involve the use of high explosives.

'There is good reason to think we know where many of the storage places for the explosives are. There remain two questions. The first: will they wait and attack simultaneously throughout the world, or will they stagger the attacks?' He paused long enough for that question to sink in, and then asked with an intensity which suggested that to him this was the most vital question of all: 'The second: should we move in on the warehouses and other known places now, before we know them all, or should we wait until all but a very few have been located? If we do that, there might be a number of attacks which could have been avoided. If we take the first course, we might successfully raid a hundred places but leave hundreds of others free to take unilateral action – and that's surely what they will do if we make a large number of raids: they'll attack one by one.'

He paused again, and after what seemed a long time, said: 'Got that, Chief Inspector?'

'Done a bit better than that, sir,' declared Pence, without showing any expression at all. 'I had it on live on our wavelength for the African Headquarters and asked *them* to relay it to all members of the International Conference. Shouldn't be too long before we start getting replies in, sir. It's far too big a decision for you to make on your own.'

As he finished, the deep tones of Big Ben floated into the room through the open window. It was half past ten. In an hour and a half Franklin's call would come, and what to decide about him would be a decision Dawlish would have to make on his own.

156

18 *Message Received . . .*

Throughout the world, senior police officers who worked with the Crime Haters and were delegates to all the Crime Haters conferences, received the message. Whether the officials were at their desks or in bed, at the theatre or at a meal, the message came through, and each one read, considered, and then took the résumé Dawlish had made to their superiors. In every case the superiors went direct to their political leaders: in Washington, to the White House, in Russia to the home of the Chairman of the Presidium, in Pekin to the Chairman of the People's Republic, in New Delhi to the Prime Minister, in Spain to the dictator – always to the highest authority.

Later, much later, when copies of the reports were studied at the Crime Haters' headquarters one thing became obvious – that the leaders had virtually asked the same questions and made much the same replies. The dictator of a small South American state who was truly benevolent and truly beloved of his people was perhaps the one whose reactions were those of the majority.

He was in bed when his Chief of Police, Generalissimo di Guarda Polizza de Farenza, a middle-aged man who knew and respected Dawlish, asked for an audience. He rose at once, put on a dressing-gown, called for coffee, and sent for the Generalissimo.

'Now, tell me, what is this grave matter?'

He listened, with a question here and there for clarification; and when it was done he sipped coffee, and asked:

'Do you know where the storehouse is here, de Farenza?'

'Yes, Excellency.'

'Is it surrounded?'

'Yes, Excellency.'

'Is there any immediate danger to the city?'

'No, Excellency – unless the explosives have already been placed in position.'

'Is there any reason to suspect that they have been?'

'No, Excellency.'

'Can we be sure there are no other storage places which we do not know?'

'We cannot be sure, Excellency.'

'So if you were to seize one there might be action from the others?'

'Your Excellency is as perspicacious as ever,' said de Farenza.

'There appears to be some perspicacity in this man Dawlish. Consider this on a global scale, de Farenza.'

'I will try, Excellency.'

The President gave a faint smile.

'Then you will eventually come to the conclusion that if we were to act with complete safety for ourselves, but before our neighbour states and others were ready, we might precipitate action which might cause our neighbours much harm.'

'That is so, Excellency.'

'However, this Mr Dawlish has not been able to state with any certainty where the attacks might come, and cannot even state with authority that there will be any such attacks.'

The Chief of Police did not answer.

'Can he?' barked the President. 'Am I not right?'

'Yes, Excellency, you are right,' de Farenza said, bowing.

'But you do not think I am sensible.'

'Until I know what you decide to do I cannot express an opinion on that,' said de Farenza, 'but I can say that I would be very surprised indeed if Your Excellency were not sensible.'

The President laughed.

'You should be a politician, not a policeman! Speak your mind, de Farenza.'

'Your Excellency is very kind.' De Farenza bowed again, even more formally. 'I can see no purpose in any group or organization building up stocks of high explosives in key cities and towns throughout the world unless they are to be used. It is conceivable that the destruction of some industrial or commerical building is being planned, but I cannot see that such a worldwide attack would serve any purpose. I can only see what it is evident that Mr Dawlish sees – the possibility of revolution, an attempt to overthrow governments of the world simultaneously. I would personally act on the assumption that this is indeed the master-plan.'

'Here, yes, it would be practicable,' conceded the President. 'I could be assassinated and another man put in my place in a matter of hours, and if the police who protect me and the armed forces also were unable to help because their weapons had been destroyed, perhaps their barracks – yes, yes. Am I reading your mind correctly, Generalissimo?'

'Perfectly, Excellency!'

'But in the great democracies the situation is very different. You do not need telling that. You would not cause a revolution in the United States by assassinating the President, or in Great Britain by assassinating either the Queen or her Prime Minister.'

'If you destroyed Parliament while it was sitting, Excellency, or destroyed the Capitol while all the senators and congressmen were there, if you destroyed the Pentagon and were able also to destroy armouries and aircraft, and if you had a trained political and military force ready to take over, able to rely on the support, for instance, of extreme right or extreme left wing, *then* – '

'It could be done,' the President finished. 'Yes, yes, I see. We shall not act alone, Generalissimo. You will tell this Dawlish that we shall act in concert with the other nations, reserving the right to take unilateral action if we are attacked or if grave international danger threatens.'

The Chief of Police bowed so low that his body was bent almost at right angles.

'I was positive your decision would be wise, Excellency,' he said, and backed towards the door. 'I will lose no time at all.'

The Commissioner of the Metropolitan Police Force, the Assistant Commissioner for Crime, and Dawlish, were together in Downing Street with the Prime Minister, who had shown a quick and welcome grasp of the situation.

'I shall have the defence forces at the ready, and all the civil defence and firefighting forces,' he said. 'If this situation changes I will call you at once, Commissioner.'

'Call the Deputy Assistant Commissioner,' advised the Commissioner. 'I shall be guided by him in any case, so by talking direct you will save time.'

The Prime Minister, a small, shy-seeming man, shook hands and smiled at Dawlish.

'I doubt if you'll ever get any official thanks for what you're doing, Mr Dawlish. I hope it helps for you to know that so many people repose so much faith in you.'

The last notes of twelve noon were striking as Dawlish entered his office after the visit to Number 10 Downing Street. Outside, the sun was at almost summer brightness although at winter height and despite open windows the empty room struck warm. He glanced at the telephone as if he expected it to ring with Franklin's call on that very moment but it stayed silent. He sat at his desk. There were piles of reports about the locating of more warehouses, there were already thirty-one acceptances from neuro-surgeons of different countries to attend the conference and listen to Mandel, while in a third file replies from chiefs of police about his assessment of the general situation were coming in. Twelve said simply: Decision rests with you. Three asked for more information. One said: Political authorities here reluctant to wait unless assured other nations will do the same.

Who could blame them?

And who, thought Dawlish, since time was so short, could possibly make a decision for him?

He riffled through individual reports and came to one from Hong Kong. It had been received in code and the decoded message was in Pence's clear handwriting; there was obviously too much going on at the office for anyone to spare time for typing.

The message read:

All the outside suppliers and home industry manu-

161

facturers who work for General Supplies Limited have now been identified, and all warehouses and the main plant of the company are completely surrounded. We are in a position to move in on instructions and are confident we can overcome all resistance.

He put this aside for a few moments, trying to think, then stood up and opened the door into the next room – Pence's room. In fact Pence worked in a corner of what had been turned into a large operations room not unlike Information at Scotland Yard, the chief difference being that everything in here communicated with overseas police forces. Twenty people were working at teletype machines and television machines, recording messages coming in by radio. Everyone seemed to be working at full pressure and with intense concentration. The only relaxed-looking person appeared to be Pence himself, who sat massive and solid with his back to Dawlish at a desk which had a row of telephones. He was speaking into one in a low-pitched voice which Dawlish could only just hear because of the noise in the rest of the room.

He replaced the receiver, turned on his swivel chair and began to get up.

'Stay where you are,' urged Dawlish, and put a hand on his shoulder. 'What do you make of Hong Kong?'

Pence pondered for a long time before he replied mildly:

'Wouldn't want to blow the whole island up, sir, would you?'

Dawlish said: 'No,' wondering, fleetingly, how often this much slower thinking man came to the same conclusion as himself. 'I'd prefer not to blow anything up.'

Pence nodded. 'No call from Franklin?'

'No, sir.'

'Any indication that anyone else at General Supplies was involved besides Tenterden?'

'No proof, sir, but there's little doubt why he was killed.'

Dawlish grunted. 'What about the men taken from The Elms?'

'Those who can talk English are unlikely to,' answered Pence, 'and short of giving them a dose of their own medicine I don't think they will.' Pence's tone was completely non-committal, Dawlish had no idea at all whether he thought the men should be put through their own particular kind of third degree, or should not.

'What about the man who shot Tenterden?' asked Dawlish.

'Officially a night-watchman at General Supplies, and by day he lived at The Elms,' answered Pence. 'He can speak English all right, complains about everything that happens, even bacon and eggs for breakfast. But not a word about anything we want.'

'Not a ghost of an inkling of the master-plot?'

'Nothing different from what you made pretty clear, sir. World-wide revolution, to be touched off simultaneously everywhere at once. Like living on the edge of a volcano, isn't it?'

Dawlish said: 'I wonder whether, if we raided the headquarters in Hong Kong, it would blow the whole city to pieces?'

Pence shrugged, and said: 'Hell of a thing to risk, sir.'

'So is world revolution,' Dawlish said as if to himself. 'Who would – '

One of the telephones on Pence's desk rang and the

older man lifted the receiver, his eyes still on Dawlish. 'Who would see himself as world leader, is that what you were going to say?' He broke off and placed the receiver to his ear. 'Who is it?' he demanded in a no-nonsense tone. Immediately his manner changed and he thrust the telephone into Dawlish's hand, whispering: 'Franklin.'

In the calmest voice he could muster, Dawlish said: 'Hallo, Justin. Come here and tell me what you want me to know and I will guarantee you can leave without trouble. That's an Old Bellyacher's promise.'

All he heard on the line was heavy breathing.

'Did he *say* he was Franklin?' Dawlish asked in an aside, and wished, as he had wished dozens of times before, that there was a way of tracing calls on automatic exchanges; computers had more to answer for than man would ever know.

'Yes, sir, he – '

'Pat,' Franklin said clearly. He seemed to be gasping for breath. 'I – I'm at – at Mandel's. I – I – '

He broke off, and the heavy breathing came again and seemed to go on for a long time before he said:

'Come and talk – come and talk to me here. I – '

He stopped, and there was a clattering sound, as if he had dropped the telephone. Pence would have heard 'Mandel's' and a car would be ready. There was more clattering before Franklin spoke again, and this time his voice was husky and sounded faraway. 'Make sure – make sure Ursula – '

Dawlish's hand was so tight on the receiver that it hurt. He could be at Mandel's clinic in twenty minutes, could have motor-cycle police clearing the road, but twenty minutes might be too long.

'Pat,' the voice came again. 'Don't – don't attack

them anywhere. Hong Kong or – anywhere. Terrible things will happen if you do. Don't – attack them.' There was a long pause, and then the voice came very faintly: 'Do you hear me?'

'Yes, Justin,' Dawlish said quietly. 'I hear you and understand.'

Silence fell, and this time it was broken by running footsteps, light enough for a woman. A voice called out: 'Sir Justin!' and there were confused sounds which Dawlish could only guess at, and a shuddering cry.

'He's dead,' Dawlish heard. 'Dear God, he's dead.'

19 *Nurses Don't Cry*

Nurses don't cry, Dawlish said to himself. Not in the course of their duty – nurses just don't cry.

'Say something, sir?' Gordon Scott was driving, Harrison was in the back, and a police car followed at a close distance while two motor-cycle police led the way without fuss or noise.

'Nurses don't cry,' Dawlish said aloud.

'I wouldn't say that, sir.'

'I suppose not,' replied Dawlish and made no attempt to explain what he meant. He leaned back with his long legs stretched out, going over in his mind all that Franklin had said. As an *aide memoire* he had a tiny tape-recorder in his pocket with a record of the conversation which Pence had taken.

Pence had the kind of invaluable mind which anticipated nearly everything.

They turned into Harley Street, and soon were drawing up outside the clinic. Another police car was already there, keeping a parking place for Dawlish. He went straight to the door which a young nurse opened. Would this be the one who had said 'He's dead! Dear God, he's dead!' No. This one looked pert and had beautiful brown eyes untouched by sorrow.

'Mr Dawlish?'

'Yes.'

'Dr Mandel is expecting you,' she said. 'If you'd come this way – '

Dawlish followed her along the corridor, Gordon Scott close behind him. Instead of going into the waiting-room the nurse led them to a door marked 12, tapped, and opened it.

'Mr Dawlish, Doctor,' she said.

Dawlish went in with Scott a pace behind him. He expected to see Justin Franklin's body, but instead he saw Ursula Franklin, his wife, lying peacefully asleep. Mandel was standing by her side.

'She is doing very well with the new treatment,' Mandel said. 'I even have hope of a full recovery.'

Dawlish asked, harshly: 'What are the chances of her husband's full recovery?'

'Mr Dawlish,' Mandel replied, spreading his hands in the mannerism which was so characteristic of him, 'he had little or no chance of survival when he arrived, not much more than an hour ago. He had been shot, as you will see, and he had his wife in the back of the car. He collapsed on the porch and we took him straight up to a room. I am not a conventional surgeon but this was an emergency and I removed a bullet from his abdomen and another from his shoulder. In rare moments of consciousness he kept saying one thing:

166

'Tell Dawlish not to attack Hong Kong.' He repeated that several times before finally going under with the anaesthetic. He came round from this much more quickly than I would have expected, and reached a telephone on the landing. We have a prepayment instrument there for patients who do not want to put their calls through on the clinic's switchboard. There a nurse found him. She had no idea whom he had called, she simply summoned me and I had him taken into the nearest unoccupied room and immediately called you. That is as much as I know, Mr Dawlish. I am grieved that he has died, but pleased – in fact highly gratified – that his wife has responded so well to the new treatment. A great new vista is opened not only to science but to many people whose minds have been turned by shock and distress and even certain kinds of injury. You will surely understand that I consider that to be of far greater importance than the death of a single human being.'

His quiet voice, impressive because of the under-emphasis and complete lack of vehemence, fell away into silence. In that moment the woman on the bed stirred, and without another word Mandel spread his arms to usher the others out of the room. Once outside Mandel drew ahead and led the way to a room further along the corridor. He opened the door, saying quietly:

'Here is Sir Justin Franklin.'

Dawlish, more used to death than most men, went slowly into the room, and his expression was bleak as he looked down at the man who had had such a fine mind. There was peacefulness in the strong face now; and repose. The head and face were unscathed, but Mandel moved forward and pulled down a sheet; in one

167

shoulder was a bullet wound, clean now, and not even bandaged or taped.

On the table by the side of the bed were two misshapen pieces of lead; the killer bullets. They lay in a small metal dish which was covered over by a transparent plastic material.

'May I take this?'

'Of course,' Mandel said.

'I've no doubt the Home Office will want an autopsy,' Dawlish said.

'I would expect them to come for the body any time,' replied Mandel.

Dawlish picked up the bullets, placed them in Gordon Scott's hand, then led the way out. He had the strangest of feelings; it was like being in the midst of life and death; between hope and despair. There was Franklin dead and Ursula alive, so much past pain and so much future promise.

'Mr Dawlish,' Mandel said as he stepped forward and touched the handle of the street door, 'have you yet any real idea why these terrible things have been happening?'

'No,' Dawlish answered, without giving a hint that this was no more than half the truth. 'Did Franklin say anything else at all?'

'Nothing, except: "Tell Dawlish not to attack Hong Kong". At first I thought he was delirious but there's no doubt at all that he was serious.' Mandel paused for a moment and then asked: 'Did you do what you promised about a gathering of the neuro-surgeons?'

'At least thirty have already promised to come,' Dawlish said.

A light passed over Mandel's face, and there seemed to be extra strength in his grip when he shook hands with Dawlish. As they went down, Gordon Scott said drily: 'Well, he's a happy man, anyhow!'

'Yes,' said Dawlish. 'The realization of a dream.' As they got into the car he went on: 'Gordon, do you know if the bullets which killed Tenterden were taken to Ballistics at the Yard?'

'I looked in and checked myself,' Scott replied.

'We'll take these there at once,' Dawlish said.

Twenty-five minutes later he was looking through the lenses at the sections of two different bullets, on an instrument so like a microscope that a layman would be unable to tell the difference. He turned the handle which would revolve one of the sections very slowly while the youthful, sandy-haired officer in charge of Ballistics stood on one side, Gordon Scott on the other.

'See, sir?' the Ballistics man asked.

'Yes. Identical markings.' So Tenterden and Franklin were killed by a bullet from the same gun. Dawlish drew back from the instrument and murmured: 'Don't attack Hong Kong.'

'What's that, sir?'

'Talking to myself – first stage of senility, don't they say?' said Dawlish. 'Very many thanks. Preserve those bullets as if they were gold, won't you?' He led Gordon Scott out, and his stride was longer as he went through the passages of the new building of Scotland Yard; Scott, tall though he was, had some difficulty in keeping up with him. As they went towards the lifts, double doors were pushed open and at least thirty men, several of them black and two of them Chinese, came out of the conference room; these were overseas visitors either on a tour, or here for a short course in what the Yard could teach them. Every eye was turned towards

169

Dawlish, who raised a hand, said: 'Good morning, gentlemen!' and passed on.

When they reached the side turning off Broadway, where their cars were parked, Scott asked:

'Had an idea, sir?'

'Yes,' Dawlish said. 'Yes. Could be a wrong one but it's an idea! We'll use the police car – could have gone to Information and done this but it would take longer, and we haven't the time.' He slid into the seat next to the driver and picked up the radio telephone. 'Information, please.' He heard the usual squeaks and groaning sounds and then the voice of the Inspector in charge of Information came through clearly:

'Information.'

'This is Deputy Assistant Commissioner Dawlish.'

'Yes, sir.'

'I want two pieces of information very quickly. They refer to the reports from the men who were watching the Mandel Clinic this morning – I want to know exactly what time visitors called, and what time ambulances delivered patients.'

'I'll call you the moment I can, sir.'

'Thanks. The second thing: I want all the information you can get me quickly about Fred Dando, the bookmaker, and whether he has any interests in Hong Kong or the Far East.'

'It's a funny thing you should ask that,' the Information officer said musingly. 'Did you know that Dando's been suspected of having favourites doped so that he can cash in when they lose?'

Dawlish said: 'No. Just suspicion?' He did not see the relevance of this but the car was speeding towards his office and there was no reason why he shouldn't half listen and think at the same time.

'Yes, sir. He's believed to plant stable boys at certain training establishments, and we've been after him for some time. The thing is, the stable boys he's supposed to have planted are English-speaking Chinese from Singapore and Hong Kong. And one of our chaps pushed this inquiry a bit further, sir. He has a big business in both places – gamble a lot, the Chinese do, apparently. But it's more than a bookmaking business – he has a general exporting business. They say he's enormously wealthy. And they're still digging for more information.'

'Bless your heart!' Dawlish exclaimed. 'Then I beg you to keep on digging!'

'I will, sir.'

'Can you put me through to the Assistant Commissioner for Crime?'

'He's not in this morning, sir, but the commander –'

'The commander will do fine.' Dawlish waited only for a few seconds before a man with a faint Yorkshire accent came on the line. This was Commander North, whom he had known for many years.

'I take it you're fully briefed, Roland,' he said.

'Anything Mr Dawlish wants, give him with both hands,' North said drily.

'Have we still a good strength at The Elms?'

'Yes – a dozen men, and there are still one or two firemen about.'

'Double the dozen,' Dawlish said, 'and have someone meet me at the house next door to The Elms in half an hour, say.'

'You mean Dando's place?' North's voice rose.

'Yes.'

'You'll never get anything on that old reprobate,'

North said. 'I – ' He broke off. 'You think there could be a tunnel from The Elms to his place?'

'Yes.'

'I'll treble the number of men,' North promised. 'Dando himself might not be there. Have you enough on him to justify a general call?'

'Not yet,' Dawlish said.

In fact, Fred Dando was at home.

There was a long delay after Dawlish, accompanied by Gordon Scott, rang the front-door bell, but at last a woman answered it; and Dawlish recognized her as one of those who had been watching from a top-floor window the previous night.

She was at least half Chinese.

She was nervous, which probably explained the expansiveness of her smile, as she said: 'Good morning,' with a fairly strong Cockney accent; Dawlish had no doubt that she was a native Londoner. 'What can I do for you, gentlemen?'

'I'd like to see Fred,' Dawlish said.

'Well, he's just going out, he's got an urgent business appointment.'

'I'm sure he will spare me a few moments,' Dawlish said. 'I want to say "thank you" for the way he helped me last night.'

'Oh, *you're* the man – Mr Dawlish, isn't it?' She opened the door wider for them to pass, but as they did so a man came hurrying from a police car. 'Fred!' called Mrs Dando. 'It's Mr Dawlish.' Scott went to see what the man wanted, while Dawlish was led into a room which he hadn't entered the previous night.

There were some beautiful pieces of oriental furniture here; a chest, a decorated screen, two vases in niches in the wall. The large carpet was Chinese with

172

the dragon pattern, even the tiles at the fireplace were oriental.

'Fred!' the woman called.

'Coming, dear!' Dando's voice sounded quite near.

Dawlish saw Scott through the open door, obviously full of the news he had just received, but Dando appeared at the same moment. Wearing a beautifully cut silk shirt and a big pearl tie-pin, he looked very different from the night before. He approached Dawlish with his hand outstretched.

'Well, what a pleasure, Mr Dawlish, ever so nice of you to look in. Lucky you caught me, I've got some conferences in London town I've got to attend, but I can spare five minutes. I can always spare five minutes for the police!' His laugh had an edge of nervousness. 'Anything special I can do for you, Mr Dawlish, or is this just a courtesy visit?'

'You can do two things for me,' Dawlish said.

'Just say the word, Mr Dawlish!'

'Thank you. You can show me the room where you kept Lady Franklin yesterday, and – '

Dando stood very still, all colour and expression drained from his face – except his eyes; and it seemed to Dawlish that there was a dangerous glitter in those eyes.

'And you can show me the way to the cellar, and where you're hiding the men who escaped from The Elms,' Dawlish said.

Dando's hand flashed to his pocket.

'Don't let him!' screamed the woman. 'He'll blow us all up!'

Dawlish struck the man on the side of the jaw with a blow which lifted his feet clear of the floor and then sent him staggering back over the dragon on the carpet.

173

Scott went forward swiftly and, before Dando had really settled, snapped handcuffs on his wrists. The woman was sobbing, face buried in her hands. Dando had a trickle of blood coming from the corner of his mouth, and was quite unconscious. With slow deliberation Dawlish went through his pockets and, in one just inside the coat and very easy of access, he found what looked like a large coin – the size of a fifty-pence piece. He took this to the woman and gripped her shoulder hard enough to make her look up. The 'coin' lay on the palm of his hand.

'Is this what he would have blown us up with?' he asked.

'Yes,' she muttered. 'There – there's a spring clip, if you open it it would blow up this whole house and everything in it. Everything.'

The entrances to connecting tunnels were found in the cellar, and there were escape holes or hatches beneath trees and shrubs in several places. In all, twenty-seven men were found and arrested, seven Chinese, two Pakistani, three Americans, two Frenchmen, a German and a Russian; the rest were English.

None of them resisted arrest.

The fingerprints of one of the Englishmen coincided with prints found at General Supplies, and bullets fired from a .32 Hakoni automatic revolver were identical to those which had killed Tenterden and Franklin. He refused to comment when charged with their murder.

Fred Dando also refused to give any information whatever, or to ask for a lawyer.

No one but the woman at Dando's house, his common law wife, would make any statement at all, and she knew little more than that there had been high ex-

174

plosives at The Elms and that Dando had extensive business dealings with General Supplies Limited as well as in hundreds of places throughout the world. She knew that he dealt in the export and import of consumer goods, but she said drearily that she had no idea what he had been planning, except that he had said that rather than be killed he would destroy himself and everyone with him, and had once shown her the 'coin' bomb.

Ursula Franklin had not been brought here, but Sir Justin Franklin had stayed in the house. He had left that morning. The woman swore that was all she knew.

'But something terrible is going to happen, Mr Dawlish, I know it is,' she said. 'For years Fred's been talking about "The Day". You caught him as he was about to start for Hong Kong to make the final arrangements.'

In Dando's pocket were air tickets, first class, to Hong Kong. He had two suitcases, ready packed. But he carried no documents of any kind, nothing that would help the police. And he would not say a word.

20 Decision

When Dawlish returned to the office, it was three o'clock.

By then all but a very few replies had come in from police and governments and the general consensus was: 'Take what action you think best.' Some said: 'Early action is essential.' There was that crushing weight of responsibility, and he kept thinking of all the factors involved, including Franklin's 'Don't attack Hong Kong.' He could find no evidence that Franklin was involved; no evidence that any of General Supplies Limited's business was unlawful, except the importing of explosives without a licence and even this had been done by members of the firm and not, as far as the police could prove, by the firm itself.

More and more reports came in of warehouses being located, until it was virtually certain that there were very few left; and each was closely watched by the police who kept their distance but could move in at a moment's notice.

'*Don't attack Hong Kong.*'

'*Early action is essential.*'

By four o'clock, Dawlish had studied all the summaries of the reports, gone over everything that could help at all, talked again with Harrison who said that Lisa could remember nothing more, talked with Mandel who said that both Mrs Gimble and Ursula Franklin were showing signs of marked improvement but it would be days before they could talk, and even then virtually certain that they would remember nothing.

'For their sake you have to pray that they will not,' Mandel said.

Dawlish said gruffly: 'That isn't the way you talked before, remember? What does the sacrifice of one or two people matter if it's for the general good?' He rang off before Mandel could answer. It was no use letting fly at the neuro-surgeon; if he let fly at anyone it should be at himself for not seeing what must surely be obvious: for being so late; for not being able to

176

make Dando talk. Before he had become a policeman he would have made Dando talk somehow or
other, but – he was a policeman.

He was sitting at the centre of one of the strangest
webs he had ever known.

Here, in London, he was in constant touch with,
virtually, all nations. Every police force in the world
was poised for action – and he was frightened to give
the signal. *Why*? He was not often, and not easily,
scared.

Why?

He heard a buzzer on his desk; Pence was on the
line. He lifted the receiver.

'Yes?'

'We've had three supplementary messages from
police sources, sir.'

'They want to move in?'

'Yes, sir.'

'I don't blame them. Come in, will you? Is Gordon
there? . . . Then bring him, too.' He swivelled round
in his chair as they entered, saying in a kind of con-
tinuation of his thoughts: 'Why am I so afraid to give
the signal to move in? Why didn't I go to Hong Kong
quickly? There isn't time to go there now before the
balloon goes up. Why am I so uncertain?'

'It's a hell of a strain,' Gordon Scott said. He looked
so young, with his well-brushed hair and his freckles;
but the anxiety in his eyes belied youth.

'I don't think it's an emotional matter at all, sir –
or one of nervous strain,' Pence said.

Dawlish looked at him beneath his frowning brows.
'What do you think?'

'It's a matter of logic, sir. You are being blocked by
what you are sure is a sound reason.'

177

'It's a sound reason that if the police forces move in they may all be blown to smithereens.'

'I don't mean that, sir,' Pence said.

'Normally, you'd take a chance,' declared Scott.

'There's some kind of mental block,' Pence said. 'You feel that if you wait long enough you will find a way of ending this affair without any more disasters.'

'Happy thought,' Dawlish said. 'It's buried deep in my subconscious if that's true. I feel as if – ' He broke off, and his whole body seemed to hunch up as if against some physical onslaught: and it stayed that way as he went on in a strained voice: 'I feel as if I've been brain-washed. As if I can't think along positive lines any more but only along negative lines. *Brain*-washed,' he repeated very softly. 'All the victims have been brain-washed in a way, and now they've got at me.'

'But it's not possible!' cried Gordon Scott.

'It is, Pence, isn't it?' asked Dawlish, softly.

Pence looked at him with a glimmer of excitement in his deep-set eyes; there was actually a quiver at his lips as he said:

'I think I see what you mean, sir.'

'I wish to hell I did!' Gordon Scott exclaimed.

'You've seen a great deal of Dr Mandel,' Pence went on, 'and you've had one or two drinks with him.'

'So I have,' breathed Dawlish. 'So I have. And it was he who said that Lady Franklin had been taken away – we never had supporting evidence. Supposing she was there all the time? And it was he who hammered in "Don't attack Hong Kong". What's more, if Franklin found this out while at Dando's place and was shot while escaping, he would get to the clinic to try to find his wife. And Mandel would tell him he would put his

178

wife through the tortures of the damned if he didn't keep me away from Hong Kong, so – '

Dawlish was already on his feet.

'This is one place where I'd like to be with you,' Pence said.

'If you'd care to come – ' Dawlish began.

'Better not, sir. In the first place it would make Mandel suspicious, and in the second it's hard enough to keep pace with the news that's coming in as it is. May I say that a signal may be expected within – well, within two hours, sir?'

Dawlish said positively: 'Yes. If I'm right about Mandel we should be able to prevent serious trouble when the police move in on the warehouses. If I'm wrong, they'll have to move in, anyhow. Come on, Gordon.'

Pierre Mandel looked very straightly into Dawlish's eyes as he said:

'I was afraid that you would find out, Mr Dawlish.'

'I've found out all right,' Dawlish said. 'Now I want to know what we can do to prevent a great deal of senseless bloodshed. I've no doubt you've one of the coin bombs and can blow us all up at the flick of your hand, but won't you be blowing up a great deal more than the Mandel Clinic and its staff and patients?'

'I do not understand you,' said Mandel, warily.

'Have you made a breakthrough in neuro-surgery and neuro-therapy?'

'Yes.'

'Do you really want to throw all that away?'

Mandel actually smiled; though not widely and not without considerable effort: nevertheless he smiled as he replied:

'You are a very ingenuous man, Mr Dawlish.'

'You may be right. But tell me, did you really plan to take over the world?'

'Yes,' said Mandel, with a sigh. 'I did indeed. It is not a very good or happy world, and the number of people in it who have some kind of brain damage or weakness is quite astonishing. It is not a world I like. I was prepared to help Dando so that he could create a kind of economic dynasty – and where better to start such a dynasty than China, from Hong Kong? – while I would control the medical and surgical situation. I would, for instance, introduce a system of euthanasia to end the misery of all who are terminally ill, all whose minds have gone, all who are crippled. I would also arrange for a compulsory form of contraception, to keep the world population to a more manageable size. I would end air and water and noise pollution – and I would do all of these things by controlling the minds of the men in my own and allied professions. Dando was to have started revolution simultaneously throughout the world, and with the threat of the uniquely powerful explosive he has discovered, hold the authorities in thrall until I was ready. And I *am* ready, Mr Dawlish, or practically so. It will take a little while, but I will shortly be able to condition the mind of men.

'That is what the experiments have been about.

'First we have selected women – and some men whom you have not yet discovered – who might be able to reveal part of what we were doing, enough at least to alert you and other police. Next, I have used many on whom to experiment, so that I can bring them back to normality. Have no doubt, I have perfected not only a cure for most damaged minds but also a way of changing man's thinking.'

180

'It could be one of mankind's great boons,' Dawlish said. 'As well as one of its greatest dangers.'

'Yes,' agreed Mandel, without hesitation. 'And it will be, and I shall direct it. You see, Mr Dawlish, if you were to give the signal to attack the warehouses and other places of importance throughout the world the explosions will do much more than destroy the attacking forces. Large sections of great cities have been mined. Schools and blocks of flats and factories – all of these will be destroyed with the people inside them. And there is no way of preventing these things from happening.'

'One way?' Dawlish asked.

'*No* way.'

'You can prevent it,' Dawlish declared.

There was a glimmer of a smile in Mandel's eyes and it moved to his lips as he spread his hands in a self-deprecating manner.

'Yes, I can,' he said. 'But I will not.' His smile broadened. 'The moment for the simultaneous explosions will come, and action will be taken unless I give a signal to delay it. I do not intend to give such a signal. If you kill me, it will not help you or the people you want to help. If you imprison me, you cannot help them. Only I can, and I will not.'

'Did Franklin know?' asked Dawlish.

'Yes, he knew. He was working with us, but when he discovered how much destruction we planned he revolted. That is why it was necessary to kidnap his wife and to submit her to ordeals which made sure she did not know the signal. That is why he eventually came to heel, returning here. That is why he pleaded with you not to attack Hong Kong: he knew the consequences of such an attack.' Mandel spread his hands in another, briefer gesture, and gave a little laugh. 'What is that homely little phrase? If you cannot beat them, join them. *Join us*, Dawlish. Have all the police withdrawn. Permit the revolt and the takeover of governments. It will prevent the bloodshed which so worries you, and it will enable everything to happen much more quickly and smoothly.'

He glanced at Scott, as if to include him in the proposal, but Scott was watching Dawlish with great intensity, as if fearful of what the other would decide, seeing no way in which good could come of any decision.

Suddenly, Dawlish chuckled; and in a moment the chuckle deepened into a laugh, as if he had suddenly seen something excruciatingly funny in the proposal. The laughter shook his whole body and puzzled Mandel as much as it puzzled Gordon Scott. He opened his left hand, and on it rested the coin bomb which he had taken from Dando, and he shifted it on to his fingers and then moved his thumb so that his nail touched the edge.

'No dice,' he said, obviously enjoying the joke hugely. 'None of the police forces will wait more than an hour or two, there's absolutely no way of preventing the disaster. So we may as well be the first to go. Gordon, get out of this place and run as fast as you can, bellowing fire. Get the clinic empty, no need for anyone else to suffer. But Mandel deserves to die because he's the most inhuman human being I've ever come across, and I deserve to because it took me so long to realize it. *Hurry*, Gordon! Bring the police in, get the staff and patients out, have the neighbourhood evacuated. I'll wait fifteen minutes, and while I'm waiting I'll see how long it takes to break every bone

182

in Mandel's body. Or better, the brain in his head.'
With his free hand he gripped Mandel by the throat.
'*Hurry, Gordon!*'

Gordon already had the door open.

Mandel gasped: 'No. No, I'll send a message.' He could hardly get the words out because of the grip of Dawlish's fingers. 'I'll send a message that it's all safe, there's a transmitter in the attic here. Don't – don't kill me, don't –'

He stood with his fingers at his neck as Dawlish let him go, and said:

'One mistake, and I'll do it. Have the place evacuated, Gordon, just in case he's as big a liar as he is a coward.'

There was a transmitter in the attic; easily approached by a narrow staircase. Mandel sent out his message and half an hour later Dawlish flashed word to every one of the delegates. It said simply:

It should be possible to act now without danger. All London leaders of the organization dead or under arrest.

Very soon, in every city and town in the world, the police moved in. And in every case they caught the saboteurs entirely unprepared.

Immediately, too, the police began to search the schools and factories, shops and office buildings where the high explosives had been planted. In some cases they were helped by members of the organization, hoping to mitigate their punishment. By the end of the day the reports which came to Dawlish were comprehensive and wholly satisfying.

Thousands of arrests had been made.

Documents showing how power was to be seized, bearing the names of those politicians willing to act for the organization, were all found.

If there were any disappointment it was among the neuro-surgeons who had been hoping to come and hear a revelation.

Papers found at Dando's home and the main office of his business showed how deeply he was involved, as also was Justin Franklin. It would be months, possibly years, before all the ramifications of the plot were fully known and stamped out. It was like a rotten tree whose root had been dug up, but whose sprawling branches and fallen leaves had still to be collected and tidied away.

'One of the saddest things is,' said Dawlish to Felicity, 'that but for his dreams of grandeur, Mandel could have been one of the world's greatest benefactors. As it is, his partner – who is not involved – knows enough of the method, and with help from copious notes Mandel has made, should be able to do what Mandel was going to do: tell the medical world of the new discovery.'

'I wonder how many of them will know how much they'll owe to you,' said Felicity. They were sitting together on the couch, arms linked, relaxed, at peace at last.

Dawlish laughed.

'I'll write an autobiography, and then everyone will know how near to failure I came.' He paused, and then said seriously: 'If I'm sorry for anyone it's for Ursula Franklin.'

'I shouldn't be,' Felicity said.

'Why not?' asked Dawlish, surprised.

'It must have been an awful strain living with Justin,' Felicity said, 'and he was too old for her anyhow. She won't remember the awful things that have happened, and she'll marry again and be happy.'

'And will Lisa Day marry young Harrison?' Dawlish asked meekly.

'If she's idiot enough to marry a policeman, yes,' Felicity said, stretching up her arms and sliding them round his neck. 'I'll have to go and see her, and warn her, of course.'

Dawlish kissed her.